THRONE OF ASHES

Stephanie Pass

For anyone who offered their hand and
set the world on fire when it bit back.

****

BOOKS BY STEPHANIE PASS

THE ENCHANTED HEART SERIES

0.5 THE ALCHEMY OF US
Available Now

1 TROUBLE OF THE MOST
WONDERFUL KIND
Available Now

2 SOMETIME AROUND MIDNIGHT
Available Now

3 THE BEACH HOUSE
Available Now

HELL OF A TIME SERIES

0.5 THRONE OF ASHES
Available Now

1 THE FIRST SIN
Available Now

2 THE SECOND COMING
Coming Soon

Content Warning

This book contains dark themes that may be distressing to some readers, including: graphic violence, torture, imprisonment, religious and infernal imagery, explicit sexual content, rough and dominant sexual dynamics, choking/breath play, spanking/impact play, degrading language during sex, blood play, manipulation within relationships, and betrayal.

***

Throne of Ashes Playlist

"Circle with Me" - Spiritbox
"A Forest" - The Cure
"Cities in Dust" - Souxisie and the Banshees
"Where is My Mind?" The Pixies
"In Your Room" - Depeche Mode
"The Summoning" - Sleep Token
"Granite" - Sleep Token
"Burn" - The Cure
"Policy of Truth" - Depeche Mode
"Spellbound" - Souxisie and the Banshees
"The Grey" - Bad Omens
"Ascensionism" - Sleep Token
"Waiting for the Night" - Depeche Mode

CHAPTER ONE

Lucifer

I didn't arrive so much as I ended up here. There was no ceremony. There was no trumpet announcing my disgrace. One moment, I was prostrate in front of The First Light with light so clean it hurt to look at, and the next, I was lying on my back in a realm that felt like an afterimage burned into reality.

Hell didn't greet me. It watched me, warily. I could feel it, the way the hairs stand up on the back of your neck when you feel eyes on your back before you ever turn around.

I walked, roaming this new creation the way immortals passed time, both slowly and all at once. That was all I knew how to do.

The ground shifted beneath my feet, like it was aware. Fire threaded through the ground and up into the air like a second atmosphere, heat breathing instead of burning.

Everywhere I went, things gave deference and moved aside, not out of fear, but expectation, like the realm itself was waiting for me to decide what I was.

I didn't decide. I didn't *want* to decide. I didn't want to be here.

I roamed through fields of ash that whispered when disturbed. There were no cities, no ruins, no structures built with intention. There was just rock, caverns, and stones. A forgotten place turned into a punishment.

The Fallen who'd followed me watched from a distance, curious, cautious, reverent in a way that made my stomach twist. The lesser ones unraveled beneath my stare, bones shrinking, limbs twisting, until they reassembled creatures that scurried away when I looked at them. And still others followed as if they had no purpose at all. They kept a respectful distance, like mourners unsure if they were allowed to approach the body.

They bowed, lowering themselves the moment I drew near. That was when I could barely stand the sight of myself.

It was like a weight lodged under my ribs. It wasn't regret, because guilt implied memory, and I had none to justify whatever this punishment was. The memory of heaven and what I had done hovered just outside my reach, a shape without a name.

As I walked, I searched myself for this pride, this ambition, this... hunger He claimed had driven me, and all I found was grief that felt fresh and raw and completely directionless. It didn't scream, it just gnawed at me.

You were meant to illuminate, not burn. It was the only thing I remembered clearly from those moments. Burned for what?

I turned those accusations over and over like a blade in my hands, searching for blood that wasn't there. If I had reached for power, I couldn't feel the grasp. If I had wanted the Throne, why did the sight of the half-formed one waiting for me to take it make me recoil? Hell offered it in glimpses, a silhouette I could just make out at the edge of my wandering. It waited patiently and accusatively, and I hated it.

The betrayal I felt for Heaven settled slowly deep within me. It took ages, like a poison that's persistent and takes its time to consume you. But from all of this, there was something I was sure of—something had been taken from me. I knew that with a certainty deeper than thought. I didn't mean my command, my place, or even my rank as an archangel. This was something different, something softer… something… essential, and the absence of it hurt more than His Light ever could.

I pressed my palm to my chest more than once, as if I might feel the shape of what was missing. All I found was ache. And anger. And a hollow place that no realm or throne or punishment could explain.

In all that time, Hell adjusted around me, quietly, waiting for me to claim it. It learned my footsteps before I learned its borders. But that ache never abated. I just learned to ignore it and kept walking, carrying my guilt like a sentence I couldn't remember, hating myself for a crime I was certain I hadn't committed. And that feeling of betrayal? It was a relentless erosion of rot, spreading through the angel I had been before I fell.

But this whole time, that desolate throne waited patiently. But I couldn't go to it. Instead, I went deeper into Hell.

I found caverns at the farthest reaches of the realm that had split and reformed and still seemed mostly raw and unshaped. I followed one narrow fissure until the rock scraped my shoulders, and the air grew still and thick. Then the passage widened without warning, opening into a vast chamber carved by time.

I stepped forward and was blinded when the Light tore through the cavern ceiling like a blade. Hell recoiled. Stone fractured. And fire withdrew.

I knew that Light. My knees almost buckled before I could stop them. The First Light descended without dimming Himself. He did not belong here, and yet the realm bent as if it knew who created it.

But He wasn't alone. In His grip was Azazael, my closest friend from before. He dragged him forward by his hair, and my breath left me. Az's wings were torn from his back, ripped as if they'd been shredded down to the bones. The wounds glowed faintly, cauterized by divinity but not healed. His body hung wrong. It was bruised, broken, and he was barely conscious.

We had been like brothers in Heaven, and I moved before I thought as The First Light shoved him toward me.

"He came to Me," He said, His voice calm and measured. "He was the one who reported your... sin." Those words struck harder than the fall had.

Azazael stumbled. I caught him. He felt too light in my arms. His head lolled back, but his eyes—his eyes were bright. Too bright. Fractured with something I couldn't decipher.

"Luc—" His voice tore on the syllable.

I searched his face for accusation or confirmation, or even betrayal. There had to be something. But I found none.

"He came to Me concerned for… your desires," The First Light continued, smirking, "for what was not yours."

I shook my head once, barely. "No."

It wasn't a denial of the charge. It was a denial of Him.

Az's fingers dug weakly into my arm. "Find…" His breath hitched. Blood dripped from the corner of his mouth. "Find the one who matters."

I leaned closer. "What?"

"Find the one who matters," he whispered again, urgency burning through what little strength he had left.

The cavern trembled.

"There is nothing for you to find," The First Light said, shaking His head as He chuckled. "There never was."

Something inside me recoiled at that. I looked up at Him. I still wanted His approval. Even then. Even with Azazael bleeding in my arms.

"What do you want me to do?" I asked.

His gaze sharpened. He glanced around the cavern, taking in the raw stone, the fractured floor, the fire withdrawing into cracks as if ashamed of itself. A faint curl of distaste touched His mouth.

"Down here," He said softly.

Az sagged more heavily in my arms.

"He is unstable," His voice was measured, almost weary. "His mind has fractured. He is spouting… nonsense."

His blazing eyes returned to mine. "And such nonsense cannot be allowed to echo."

The cavern seemed smaller beneath His gaze. "He must be contained," He said. "You must contain him."

The implication hung between us, sharp as judgment. *Down here.*

This was the realm I had earned. This was the consequence of my pride. If Azazael was broken, then he belonged with the broken. If he was tainted, then he belonged with the tainted. With me.

The First Light stepped closer, not enough to touch the stone, not enough to dirty Himself with it. "I trust you understand," He said quietly.

He didn't explain further. He didn't need to. This was instruction. Correction. This was proof that I hadn't been abandoned entirely. If He still entrusted me with something, then I wasn't beyond repair. I could still obey and be useful.

I shifted Azazael's weight in my arms and lifted my chin. "I will see to it," I said.

The words felt steady. But as the First Light

lingered, as His gaze held mine, something inside me faltered. And for a single, treacherous heartbeat, I almost said it. I almost asked.

Am I forgiven?

The question pressed against my teeth, fragile and humiliating. I swallowed it. If I did this well—if I obeyed without hesitation—He would not need to say it aloud. He would know I was still His. He would see that I could still illuminate.

The First Light's expression did not soften. But He inclined His head. And I took that as enough. His Light withdrew, but it wasn't gentle. When it tore back upward, the cavern ceiling sealed like a wound closing, and Hell exhaled in a low rumble.

It felt darker than before, and Az sagged against me when He vanished, as if whatever had been holding him upright had gone with it. I adjusted my grip, careful not to press against the torn remnants of his wings. His blood was warm against my hands. Too warm. It soaked into the ash at my feet and vanished without a trace.

Contain him. The word echoed, and Hell shifted beneath us, a low tremor running through the stone like it was listening.

Where was I to take him? I had no idea, so I walked. Deeper. Away from the place the

Light had wounded. The caverns twisted and narrowed as I moved through them, passages sloping downward, the air growing humid.

Az's breath came shallow against my shoulder, and he stirred again.

"Luc…" he murmured.

I didn't answer. I couldn't afford to.

The rock changed the further we went. It grew smoother. Less fractured. As though something had shaped it long ago and then abandoned the effort. I followed a narrow descent until the floor dropped away into darkness.

I kept going until it opened up, and at the center of a vast hollow in the stone was a structure. It had not been built by hand. It had grown. A circular shaft, sheer and precise, cut straight down into blackness. There were no ledges or handholds. The walls were too smooth to climb. Too deep to measure. Heat breathed faintly from within it, but no light returned.

A natural oubliette. A place designed for forgetting. Hell had made it without instruction. Or perhaps it had always been waiting.

Azazael stirred again as I approached the rim. His fingers curled weakly into my shoulder.

"Lucifer," he breathed, and for a moment,

his gaze cleared, sharp and lucid through whatever damage had been done to him.

"There's someone—" His voice faltered. A flicker crossed his face, not in confusion, but in interruption. "She—" The word tore free of him.

And something inside my chest answered. It wasn't a memory. It was an impact. There was a sharp, visceral pull in my belly, like a cord snapping taut. My breath hitched before I could stop it. For a fraction of a second, the cavern disappeared—the ache I'd been carrying since the fall sharpened into something almost recognizable.

Almost.

Azazael gasped as if struck. His head jerked slightly, eyes flashing with pain that wasn't physical. "Find..." he forced out, teeth clenched. "Find the one who matters."

That pull twisted again, not toward him. It was past him, toward something I couldn't see.

I gripped his shoulder harder than I meant to. "Who? Who are you talking about?"

He swallowed, blood darkening his mouth. "They took—" The sentence died. His eyes widened, not with madness, but with fury. "She matters," he whispered. "More than—"

The rest vanished. And I felt it then. Not the words. An absence—like something had been there and was ripped cleanly away. The ache in my chest recoiled, folding in on itself. I shoved it down. Forced it back into whatever hollow it had been gnawing at since I fell.

This was delirium. Trauma. Divine punishment. This wasn't truth. And when the command echoed again—*contain him*—I didn't argue.

Az didn't resist when I carried him closer toward the pit. He didn't fight me.

He only said it once more, barely a breath. "Find her."

And this time it hit like a blow. For a heartbeat, I almost asked why that hurt. Then I told myself it didn't.

He sagged against me.

"Forgive me," I murmured. I don't know which of us I meant.

He only whispered it again. "Find the one who matters."

I told myself it was madness, that obedience would fix this, that this was mercy, and I would be forgiven. He might be forgiven.

And then, I lowered him carefully to the edge. For a moment, I almost stopped myself. The ache in my chest flared again, sharp and unreasonable. Something inside me clawed toward him, toward whatever unfinished warning hung in his broken voice. But I silenced it.

"You will be safe here," I told him, but I didn't know if I meant it.

His hand slipped from my shoulder. "Find the one who matters," he whispered.

Then I let go. He didn't scream as the darkness swallowed him whole. The sound of his body striking the depths came long after he vanished from sight.

I stood at the rim of the pit for a long time, and it seemed as if the entirety of Hell went still, holding its breath, like we were both waiting for something—forgiveness, justification, maybe even relief. But none came. There was just that fucking hollow in my chest. Then I stepped back from the rim.

My gaze drifted over the stone until I found what I needed, a slab of rock half-embedded in the cavern floor. It was heavy, but it took little effort to pry it loose. Hell yielded to me like it always had.

I dragged it across the ground, the scrape echoing down the shaft. The sound went on too long. I told myself he wouldn't notice it, that he was already too far below. That he'd been barely conscious when I let go.

I positioned the stone over the mouth of the pit and pushed. It sealed the opening with a final, decisive weight. The cavern shifted as it settled into place, edges fusing enough that fingers could not find purchase beneath it.

He was contained. He wasn't dead. Because it took a lot more than this to kill an angel. He was contained, I reminded myself, just like The First Light had asked of me.

I stood over it for a moment, staring at the flat surface as if it might answer me. Then I began to gather the loose stones scattered around the cavern floor—one by one. I placed them over the slab, not because it was necessary, but because it felt like my penance.

Each rock landed with a dull thud.

Each one said, "Obedience."

Each one said, "Forgiveness will come."

My hands were steady, but my jaw wasn't. I imagined the First Light watching. He was measuring, judging. I imagined His approval descending like warmth, like absolution. But it didn't come. It never did.

Instead, something colder slid into place inside me. With every stone I stacked, that pit under my ribs widened quietly.

Azazael had trusted me. We'd had each other's backs for millennia and now...

The memory of his fingers gripping my shoulder flashed through my mind. The clarity in his eyes. The way he had practically begged me to find *her*, as if it meant some kind of salvation.

I pressed another stone into place. *This was mercy,* I told myself. This was discipline. This was necessary.

When the last of the loose rocks was piled high enough that the opening disappeared entirely, I stepped back. The surface looked natural now. Unremarkable. Like it had always been part of the cavern floor.

Forgotten. *Lethe Nomatos.*

My hands were stained dark. I didn't wipe them clean. And for a fleeting, treacherous moment, I wished he had fought me or cursed me or even called me a monster. But he hadn't. He had just asked me to find *her.* Something in my chest flared again, sharp and unwelcome, and I crushed it.

The First Light would be pleased. He would see that I had obeyed. He would know.

But the silence that followed felt absolute. And then somewhere deep below the stones, beyond reach, something shifted. I had just taken three steps toward the cavern mouth when I heard it.

It sounded like a knock, faint. So faint I almost mistook it for the settling of stone. A dull, hollow tap from somewhere beneath the slab.

I stopped, and the cavern held its breath again.

Then another sound followed. Softer. Uneven. Like knuckles striking rock without strength behind them. My spine went rigid.

It would be easy to move the stones. Easy to lift the slab. Hell would yield if I commanded it to.

The knock came again. It didn't seem frantic or desperate. It was measured. As if he knew I was still there.

My jaw tightened until it ached. "This is containment," I said aloud, though there was no one but me to hear it.

I took a step back. There was only silence. And then—

Tap. A pause. Tap.

Something in my chest lurched in answer. A reflex. A pull. The same sharp, unreasonable cord that had tightened when he said she.

I stepped again toward the pile before I realized I was moving. My hand hovered over the topmost stone. Just one shift. Just one breath of doubt.

The First Light's voice echoed in memory. *He must be contained.*

That pit inside me widened, but the knock didn't come again. I waited for it. I told myself I was waiting to ensure the seal held. But I was lying.

When the silence stretched long enough to become truth, I lowered my hand. If he lived, he would adapt. If he survived, he would endure. That was mercy. It was discipline. It was obedience.

I forced my feet to move. Each step away felt heavier than the slab I had dragged into place. Behind me, the cavern returned to stillness. The stones settled. There was no more knocking. Only the faint hum of Hell breathing again.

And beneath it all, too deep to measure, something had begun to fracture inside me. I told myself it was guilt. I refused to name it what it really was—grief.

CHAPTER TWO

Lucifer

Hell still didn't feel like mine, not even after thousands of years of being trapped inside it. I hadn't ruled it, not really. I hadn't claimed it. I'd wandered through it like a ghost with a title I refused to answer to, sulking in the long, petulant way only immortals can manage. It felt like a punishment dressed in velvet, a kingdom built to mock what I'd lost, a throne carved out of consequence that I wouldn't touch out of spite.

The stone beneath my bare feet was always warm but never comforting. The air tasted of iron and old smoke, as if someone had struck a match in a sealed room and let it burn for centuries to see what would remain. I'd walked through it endlessly, corridors and caverns and broken halls that blurred together, carrying my anger like a second set of wings.

Above me, there was no real sky, only the suggestion of one with clouds of soot and a dark amber ball of light that breathed like a lung. Somewhere far off, something screamed, then quieted, then screamed again, like it was practicing what it meant to belong here.

Ash still clung to my wings in stubborn, humiliating patches. I could feel it in the joints, a grittiness that clung to me, the residue of Heaven's fire casting me out but still refusing to let me go.

My light, once the brightest, the most pristine thing, refused to rise the way it used to. It flickered in fits, like it didn't trust my body anymore, like it had learned some new rule since I fell and hadn't bothered to tell me.

I remembered the Throne in Heaven, the way the air had snapped with judgment, the way my name had sounded in His mouth.

Lucifer. Morning Star. Lightbringer.

I remembered the anger He had, the weight, the thunder, and my stomach turned. But the words.. I couldn't remember. What He said had faded like memories worn through, like trying to hold water in a fist. He said I wanted to be Him. *To be... Him?*

I had never... never wanted that. It didn't spark recognition, satisfaction, or even shame.

It felt like hearing a rumor about myself from someone who had always hated how brightly I burned.

I could accept His cruelty. I could accept my punishment. I could even accept exile. But being rewritten? Something I was sure wasn't true? That was the one thing I just couldn't swallow.

I dragged a hand through my hair and laughed once, sharp and humorless. The sound echoed off the stone, lonely and lost, and it pissed me off even more.

I stood at the edge of the dais and stared at the throne that had been made for me. It hadn't always looked like this. In the beginning, it had been half-formed — a jagged rise of black stone pushed up from the floor, rough and uneven, more wound than seat. It hadn't offered comfort. It had offered accusation.

But Hell was patient. And so was I.

Over a millennium, the stone refined itself. The edges sharpened. The back rose higher, arching like a spine growing accustomed to bearing weight. Molten gold began to vein through it, not poured, not placed, but earned, seeping upward as if drawn by the pressure of my rule.

It wasn't a gift. It was a verdict.

It was beautiful in the way an executioner's

blade was beautiful, polished, deliberate, and designed to look inevitable. Armrests carved into the suggestion of claws that seemed ready to close around whoever dared sit. Even the crown hovering above it felt like a mockery, my halo inverted and suspended in heat.

It had started as punishment, but it had become proof. And now it looked like it had always belonged to me.

But I turned away from the throne because if I looked at it much longer, I was going to tear it apart with my bare hands. And I refused to give Heaven the satisfaction of my performing like a wounded animal in a cage.

That was when the air changed. It wasn't the heat. Hell, for the most part, was always hot. It wasn't the smell. Brimstone was a constant stench of sulfur and smoke. It wasn't the creatures who'd lingered near the dais, unsure what their purpose here was.

This was something else, something floral and ancient, like a Garden that had learned how to bite—Gardenia and Myrrh, and a hint of smoke that didn't belong to my fire.

I stilled, rolling a lick of flame through my fingers. The space behind me felt occupied, not by weight, but by presence, by the kind of confidence that didn't ask permission to exist.

I didn't turn right away. I let the silence

stretch until it felt like a threat, and then I looked.

She stood at the base of the dais like she'd always belonged there, like she was admiring a home she intended to redecorate. Dark hair, pale skin kissed by defiance, red silk that clung to her as if it understood exactly what kind of sin it was trying to advertise.

Lilith didn't bow. She didn't kneel, not to me. She tilted her head, her eyes tracking the ash flaking off my wings like she was reading a story written in soot.

"So," she said, her voice velvet over steel, "this is where He put you."

I stared at her for a long beat, letting my expression go flat, because I wasn't going to give her the pleasure of seeing how much I needed anything that looked like familiarity.

"Adam finally got bored with you?" I asked.

Her mouth twitched, not quite a smile, not quite a snarl.

"Adam got bored with a woman who wouldn't pretend she was made to serve him," she said, and the words didn't sound like heartbreak. They sounded like a blade being sharpened.

I took one step down from the dais, then another, meeting her on the same level. Not because I feared her, but because I refused to speak to her from above. Not even in Hell.

"You refused," I said.

"I laughed in his face," she corrected, and her eyes flashed. "Then I left."

There was a beat where we just looked at each other, two creatures holding the same shape of rejection in different hands. I had been cast down. She had walked away.

It should've made us enemies, two egos in one room, but something else hummed beneath it, something older than pride. Understanding. Power. Pain.

Lilith's eyes searched my face, and I knew she saw it, too. The flare of recognition, the way something old and dangerous stirred beneath my skin.

"He gave him another," I said, before I could stop myself.

She tilted her head. "Another what?"

I held her gaze. "Another mate."

Understanding flashed, quick and bright. She nodded as she swallowed. "Eve," she said.

My pulse reacted before my mind could, a quiet hitch, like I knew that name intimately, and it made no sense.

"Like I was a mistake He could edit out," she scoffed. "Like my obedience could be grown from dust and ribs and expectations."

She leaned in then, close enough that her

breath brushed my cheek, warm and scented and infuriatingly steady. "Doesn't He always replace what refuses Him?" she asked.

The fire around us hissed louder, reacting to something in my chest I wasn't controlling particularly well. I stepped back, breaking the closeness, turning toward the throne again. The damned thing loomed with its sharp edges and molten veins.

"I guess He expects me to sit," I said. "To be grateful He gave me a kingdom instead of nothing."

I lifted a brow as I stared at it, "Isn't it odd, though? He accuses me of trying to take His Throne, and then gives me one?"

Lilith looked past me to the throne, and her hunger showed, not for the seat itself, but for what it promised. I realized too late that she wasn't hearing my doubt. She was hearing an invitation.

"You look lonely," she said softly as she ran her fingertips down my arm, and it was the most dangerous thing she'd said yet.

I let my smile show, slow and sharp. "I look busy."

She stepped closer, close enough that I could smell the Gardenia clinging to her skin like a dare, and her presence pressed in like a hand against my throat.

"Are you going to sit up there like a good

little king," she murmured, "and pretend this was what you wanted?"

Something went hot in my chest, the anger rising so fast it almost felt like relief. This was not what I wanted. I never wanted this.

I leaned in, just enough, and said, "I never wanted His throne," I said. "I wanted…"

Something shifted in my chest, not a memory, more like the outline of one.

"I wanted to be something He couldn't control."

Lilith's eyes widened a fraction, then softened into something like satisfaction.

"There you are," she whispered, like she'd come all this way to find that exact sentence.

I stared at her for a long moment, then glanced back toward the throne that waited like an insult. When I looked at her again, my decision was already made. Not because she'd persuaded me, but because she'd reminded me that I wasn't the only one who refused to kneel.

I extended my hand, palm up in an offer. "There's room for you," I said. "The throne doesn't have to be mine alone."

Her smile returned, slow as smoke. "And what do you want in exchange, Morning Star?" She didn't take my hand.

I held her gaze and let the darkness in my voice deepen, the part of me that had learned what I could do down here from the moment I arrived. Hell only respected what could destroy it.

"I want," I said, "someone who understands what it is to be punished for refusing to be small."

Lilith's smile sharpened, slow and dangerous, and I stepped closer. I was not gentle. My hand closed around the back of her neck, fingers threading into her hair, tilting her head back just enough that the firelight caught in her eyes.

A quiet ripple moved through those lounging near the base of the dais, every creature watching to see which way the balance would tip.

Her breath caught, not in protest, but in interest.

"You think you came here broken," I said softly, my thumb brushing along her jaw as I held her there. "But you didn't fall."

I leaned closer, close enough that my words belonged only to her. "You were unleashed."

For a heartbeat, the throne room held its breath. Then Lilith laughed, low and pleased, her hands sliding up my arms like a queen accepting a challenge she had been waiting for.

"Yes," she murmured. "That will do nicely."

I let her go, raising my palm again, and this time, she immediately placed her hand in mine like she'd been waiting for it her entire existence. Her skin was cool, and the moment our fingers met, the room seemed to inhale.

She stepped past me, toward the dais, toward the throne, and for one treacherous second, I felt something like triumph. It wasn't love or peace. It was the intoxicating relief of not being alone in my exile.

She let go and started climbing, the red silk trailing behind her like spilled blood. She didn't sit. She stood beside the throne, one hand resting lightly on its arm, claiming space without claiming position.

I slowly followed her up to the dais.

"They tell stories," I said. "About me. About you. Stories that make them look clean."

Lilith looked back over her shoulder, eyes gleaming. "Stories can be rewritten."

The word rewritten made something in my skull ache, a pressure I couldn't quite place, like a memory knocking on a locked door.

She studied my face for a moment, weighing something I couldn't see.

"I won't kneel again," I said as I let the darkness seep in again, "not to Him."

I hesitated. Trust had not survived the fall with me. It lay somewhere in Heaven's realm with everything else I'd lost. But she stood there with the same fire in her eyes that burned under my ribs, the same quiet refusal to bow to a god who had cast us both aside.

Slowly, I turned my hand over, offering again as my fingers flexed once, as if testing the shape of the choice before I made it permanent.

She noticed. Of course she did, and then her mouth curved, satisfied but careful not to show it too openly. Then she raised her hand, palm up to mine, and slid her fingers into mine.

"Then," she said softly, "let's rule."

The fire in the pits surged. Somewhere deep beneath us, Hell shifted, learning a new name for its loyalty. Anger wrapped around me again, and I told myself it was armor. I didn't realize I'd just shown her where it opened.

CHAPTER THREE

Lucifer

The fire didn't settle when she approached the throne. It leaned. The stone beneath it shifted with a low, resonant sound, not a groan but a recognition, and the throne widened of its own accord. Those sharp seams softened, the armrests stretching until there was space for her without an invitation or a command. That unsettled me more than I wanted to admit.

Hell noticed her. Not just this place, but its living will. The whole realm recalibrated around her presence, pressure changing in the air itself, the heat redistributing like a living thing adjusting to a new center of gravity. Currents of fire bent toward her. The throne never demanded my weight, but it welcomed hers, responsive in a way it had never been to me.

Across Hell, movement stilled. Shadowy

things paused mid-stride, their attention snapping sharp as if a new constant had been introduced into their reality. They turned as one, desire sharpening into focus, hunger recognizing a kindred axis. Shades gathered at the edges of the light. Whisperers fell silent. Creatures throughout the realm stopped and took measure.

I stood beside the throne, one hand resting on the arm, like I might tear it free if it dared betray me. But Lilith noticed. She noticed everything.

"Careful," she murmured, eyes on the fire curling along the floor. "If you don't sit soon, they'll start wondering if you intend to rule at all."

"Let them," I said. "It doesn't matter." I said as I raised my chin, "And fear works better when it's unanswered."

She smiled faintly, approving.

Below us, shapes shifted in the gloom. The damned didn't speak, didn't kneel, didn't dare approach. They watched, measured, waiting to see whether this new King would fracture under the weight of Hell or if I would finally take a stand and reshape it in my image.

Lilith stepped closer, close enough that the silk of her dress brushed my arm.

"You're bleeding," she said.

I glanced down instinctively, then scowled. "I'm not."

"Not visibly," she agreed. "But your power is raw. Unanchored. Hell feels it. So do I."

I turned toward her sharply. "You came here for something."

Her gaze met mine without flinching. "Of course I did."

"And now you share a seat with me," I said. "Isn't that enough?"

"For now," she said lightly.

That phrase scraped.

She walked a slow circle around me, fingers trailing just close enough to my wings that I could feel the heat shift. She wasn't touching me. She was mapping.

"You're still newly fallen," she said. "Which makes you volatile. Dangerous. Magnificent." Her eyes lifted to mine. "But also vulnerable."

I bristled. "I don't need—"

"No," she cut in smoothly. "You don't need protection. You need permanence."

She stopped in front of me again. "Do you know what happens to unbound power in places like this?"

I didn't answer.

"It devours it," she continued. "Or breaks it. Or... teaches it obedience through attrition." Her lips curved. "Often, all three."

I laughed once, sharply. "Let it try."

Lilith studied me for a moment, then reached out and placed two fingers lightly over my pulse. I should have stopped her, but I didn't.

"There," she said softly. "You feel that?"

I did. There was a subtle drag, like my power hesitating before answering me fully.

"You were tossed here, a king without roots," she said. "A throne without a foundation. That makes you easy to isolate."

Anger flared. Familiar, but comforting.

"And you," I said, voice low, "are offering to fix that."

"I'm offering to share the cost," she corrected.

She withdrew her hand and met my gaze squarely. "You and I are both outliers. We both refused the shape He wanted us to take. And now we're here, in a system made to punish."

"What are you proposing?" I said.

"A binding," she replied.

The word landed with weight. She didn't want a marriage, and I was sure she had no interest in love. This would be different.

I narrowed my eyes. "I'm not taking a binding lightly."

"Good," she said. "Neither do I."

She stepped closer again, close enough that her presence pressed against my chest. "A mutual tether. Power braided, not stolen. Your authority would be anchored through me. My survival would be guaranteed through you."

"And the cost?" I asked.

Her smile was slow. Calculating. She shook her head. "We just become harder to erase."

I searched her face, looking for deception, manipulation, some obvious hunger for control. There had to be something. Lilith was known for her cunning. But… I found none.

What I found instead was something colder. Practicality. And maybe that would do, for now.

"You don't trust me," I said.

"I trust a binding," she replied, dipping her chin. "Trust comes later. Sometimes."

The fire around us flared, reacting to the tension coiling between us.

"If I bind with you," I said carefully, "Hell will recognize it. It will recognize you. Officially."

"Yes."

"And Heaven will notice."

"I would hope so," she quipped.

"And if I ever want out—"

Her gaze sharpened. "You won't."

The certainty in her voice should have alarmed me. Instead, it steadied something in my chest. I looked down at the throne again, in the way it waited. In the way, everyone had already decided what I was supposed to be.

"I won't be alone in this," I said.

"No," Lilith agreed softly. "You won't."

She extended her hand this time, palm up, mirroring my earlier gesture. "A binding," she said. "Not of obedience. Of refusal."

The word thrummed through me. *Refusal.* And it settled into me in a quiet satisfaction, like a promise I intended to keep.

I took her hand. The heat surged immediately, power reacting instinctively, the fire drawing closer as if it were waiting for a sign.

Lilith's fingers tightened, deliberate and precise. "Blood," she said.

I bared my teeth in a grin that tasted like violence. "Of course."

I drew a dagger from my belt and dragged it across my palm without ceremony. Fire stirred at me as my blood welled, dark, almost black. Smoke drifted, coiling around the cut like it was considering something. It was like deciding whether to close the wound or leave it open. I watched it waver and wondered, briefly, if it was trying to warn me, but I didn't pull away.

Lilith didn't hesitate. She mirrored the motion with a blade she pulled from her thigh. It looked older than metallurgy, the way its edge sang softly as it cut. Her blood wasn't dark like mine. It was lighter, cooler, almost luminous, like something ancient that didn't beat or breathe, carrying a scent like a cool pine that caught in my chest and made my head tilt.

She stepped closer and pressed her palm against mine. And suddenly, the realm shifted, but it wasn't violent. It felt structured and methodical as the power braided between us.

It wasn't a merging exactly. It was like a… rerouting, like two rivers forced into the same canyon and told they would share its shape forever. Hell reacted instantly as our blood mingled together. The fires roared in satisfaction. The molten veins in the throne blazed as if they were bearing witness to something new.

I sucked in a sharp breath as something locked into place inside my chest. It wasn't painful. It was a new connection, and it settled with terrifying precision, a click I felt more than heard, like a mechanism finally engaging after eons of waiting.

Her eyes opened, clear and sure. "There," she said. "You're not a single point anymore.

We're paired."

The fire eased and soothed without extinguishing as Hell exhaled. I flexed my fingers slowly, testing myself. Power answered immediately, clean and whole, no hesitation, no drag. The relief that followed was so sharp it almost felt like pleasure.

I let out a quiet laugh. "That's it?"

"For now," Lilith said.

That scraped under my skin, like I'd been exposed. I had already given Hell everything — my hands, my will, my attention.

"Hell needs two anchors." Lilith's lips brushed against my ear as she whispered, "True equals."

She stepped back and released my hand slowly, like she was making a point of it. But our new bond didn't loosen. If anything, it hummed, a quiet undercurrent beneath my skin, aware of her even when she stepped away from me.

"If you want more," she said, already turning away from the throne, "then, this was just the foundation, and our binding needs to be completed… fully."

I followed her without thinking, through corridors that rearranged themselves at my approach. Hell was bending like it was eager to please. My rooms waited at the end, vast and unused, stone and shadow and firelight arranged into something that resembled rest.

Lilith paused at the threshold and looked back at me, her expression gentler than I expected. "We're bound, but we can become more," she said quietly. "They cast us both out for the same reason, didn't they? Because we wouldn't bend."

Her fingers brushed the door frame, lingering. "But the bond..." Her eyes met mine, "It isn't finished yet. It settles when we choose each other fully."

My pulse ticked once, hard. "And what does that cost?" I asked.

Her smile was slow, knowing, already intimate with the answer. "Nothing you haven't given before," she said. "Just... you. And..."

She didn't wait for my answer as she slid her fingers into my belt loops and pulled me in, decisive and sure, like she'd already accounted for the distance between us. I let myself go easily, a smile curving before I could stop it, sharp and reckless and entirely unguarded.

"If Heaven ever looks down here again," she murmured, close enough that her words brushed my mouth. "Shared power looks less threatening."

Her hands stayed where they were, grounding me, anchoring me in a way this place never had. The bond stirred immediately, that same hum beneath my skin, responding to her proximity. I could feel her through it now, clearer than before, not her thoughts, but her certainty.

She tilted her head, studying my face, reading the way my pulse betrayed me. "You're still waiting, bracing," she observed. "Like you expect this to be taken from you."

"Old habit," I said lightly.

She smiled at that, slow and knowing, and stepped closer until there was no space left to negotiate. Her body was cool against the heat rolling off mine, a contrast that made my breath hitch despite myself.

"This isn't about taking," she said. "It's about letting this bond settle into flesh."

Her fingers slid over my chest, slow and seductive as the flames along the walls responded, curling closer, attentive, as if they understood something was being decided.

I lifted a hand and hesitated for half a second, then rested it at her waist. The contact sent a quiet jolt through the tether, warmth threading up my arm and into my chest.

"Let this be the first thing that's ours," I said again, lower now.

Lilith's gaze flicked to my mouth, then back to my eyes. "You don't have to pretend this is strategy," she said softly. "You're allowed to want it."

The honesty of that caught me off guard.

She leaned in then, slow enough that I could have turned away, her lips brushing mine in a kiss that felt less like a conquest and more like confirmation. "I want it. I want.. you."

Her mouth was cool, deliberate, and unhurried. The bond surged in response, power tightening, aligning, the connection settling deeper with each heartbeat. I felt it take root, the binding threading itself through muscle and breath and heat, no longer just an idea, but a presence.

When she pulled back, her fingers were wrapped around my shoulders, her forehead resting briefly against my chest. I exhaled slowly and let myself be pulled the rest of the way in, the door sealing behind us with a quiet finality that made the bond hum low and restless beneath my skin.

Her gaze traveled my face, my throat, and finally stopped on the place where my pulse beat too visibly now, hunger etched on her face. The fire along the walls flared and then dimmed, leaning closer.

"You seem different," she murmured. "More settled."

I huffed a breath. "You say that like it's a compliment."

"It is," she replied softly. "Your power will behave better when it knows where it belongs."

Her hand slid down my spine, her cool fingers tracing slowly and leaving awareness in their wake. I caught her wrist before I realized I'd moved. She didn't resist.

Our eyes met, something sharp and knowing passing between us. "You're still deciding," she said.

"No," I replied, voice low. "If I were still deciding I wouldn't have agreed to the binding. I wouldn't have let you lead me here. I'm just… noticing the consequences."

"And?" She asked.

I traced the line of her shoulder slowly, my fingers catching the delicate straps of her silk gown and easing them down. I leaned closer, drawn by the quiet way she let me near. My mouth brushed her throat, and then the top of her shoulder, a lingering kiss meant more as reverence than hunger.

"He tried to make you smaller, so he wouldn't feel threatened by you," I said quietly, the words warm against her collarbone. I felt her pulse flutter beneath my lips and the way she stilled as if no one had ever said it aloud before.

"But you weren't made to shrink," I murmured, lifting my head just enough to look at her. "You were made to stand beside power, not bow to it."

The fabric of her dress whispered as it dropped off her body, into a pool at her feet, and she shivered beneath my touch.

Her lips curved. "Yes."

She stepped out of it and into me, closer than before, her body fitting against mine like the space had been waiting for her. The contrast was dizzying, her coolness against my heat, shadow against fire. I could feel the bond tightening, sinking deeper, no longer abstract but physical.

She tilted her head, exposing the line of her throat, and the sight tugged something instinctive and feral out of me, a reflex I didn't bother to suppress as my cock hardened and pressed into her stomach.

"You're burning," she whispered with a smile against my lips.

"I think you like me this way."

Her mouth found mine again, slower this time, deeper, the kiss unspooling rather than striking. Not conquest. Invitation. My hand slid to her waist without thought, anchoring myself as the bond surged, power rolling through me in thick, intoxicating waves.

My other hand slid up into her hair. I wrapped it around my fist and gave it a tug. Her breath hitched as her eyes found mine.

For a moment, there was nothing else, no throne, no Fall, no Heaven watching from above, just heat and proximity and the dangerous relief of being wanted as I was.

I pushed her back onto the bed and followed, bracing myself over her, the space closing until there was nowhere for either of us to pretend this wasn't happening. Heat rippled through me, answering the bond, the way her gaze never wavered.

We kissed, her hands in my hair, nails dragging down my scalp. I growled, snapping my fingers, and my belt and trousers vanished in a rush of smoke and heat curling up my spine like approval as my wings flared out.

She pulled back just enough to smirk. "You've got tricks…"

I arched a brow as I pressed closer, letting her feel exactly how little patience I had left. "Do I?" I murmured.

Whatever restraint I'd arrived with burned off fast. I took her mouth again, rougher now, all teeth and intent, letting urgency replace anything that might have passed for gentleness. I sank deep into her cool center, giving her no time to adjust to my size before I began to pump in and out of her. Her fingers tightened against my back as I leaned down, capturing her nipple between my lips, tasting the shiver that ran through her.

Her back arched up, moaning as her hands slid down to grip my biceps and grind her clit against my pubic bone as I met her. We moved together as one, until she threaded her fingers through my hair and yanked my head back. I let go of her nipple with a loud pop.

Her eyes found mine. "Lucy, baby," She moaned, "I need more… Harder. I need… to come. Now."

I stilled, and my cock twitched inside of her. "Say please."

She scoffed, but there was mischief in her eyes as she cooed, "Please. Lucy."

I sat up and flipped her over like a rag doll, and entered her wet coolness in one fell swoop, and began pounding her from behind. I pulled her up to her knees, wrapping my hand around her waist.

With each thrust, I growled, "Is. This. What. You. Need?"

"Fuck… yes…" Her breath stuttered.

This was the most undone I'd ever seen Lilith, and I liked it. I wanted to see it again and again.

I was barely holding on, but I wrapped her long, dark hair around my fist again, twisting it tight against her skull as I continued to pound her from behind.

I let go of her waist and raised my hand,

slapping her ass hard enough to leave a mark. She gasped, and I felt her inner muscles clench against my cock. I did it again and again, until her ass cheek turned bright red, and a gush of liquid ran down my balls.

"You like that, you dirty slut?" I asked, as I continued to ravage her.

"Yes… do it again…" she moaned, and her walls began to flutter against me. She was close, and so was I.

"Who's your king?" I asked as I spanked her again.

She spluttered, "You," as her breath broke around the answer.

I let go of her hair and leaned down, wrapping my hand around her throat and gripping it, giving myself better leverage as I stroked even deeper.

I let power seep into my voice as I whispered against her ear, "Say. My. Name. Who is your king?"

"Lucifer…" She choked out just before she shattered and screamed into the pillows.

The world narrowed to heat and breath and the way the bond flared brighter with every movement, every sound, every stolen inch between us. She clenched around me, and I couldn't hold it any longer as ecstasy flowed through me and I flooded her with my seed.

After a moment, I rolled off her, out of

breath, and she raised her head and looked over at me, grinning, before sitting up on her knees.

Before I knew it, she was over me, sliding down my still pulsing cock as her smile turned sharp. She leaned over and kissed me again. Then, her lips drifted from my mouth, down my jaw, straight to the pulse at my throat.

"Don't tell me you're already tired, Lucy." She chuckled.

I felt her pause there, breath cool against my skin, her fingers tightening slightly on my shoulder. Something razor-fine ran against my throat as the bond flared, something sharp and eager leaning forward, curious.

My hands came up around her as I swallowed. "Lilith—"

"Hush," she said gently as she slowly began to ride me. "This part requires trust."

Her mouth brushed my pulse, barely there, just enough to make my breath hitch, and then she ran her tongue against it. I felt it then, unmistakably, the shift in her to a predator, the way hunger sharpened into focus.

It wasn't lust. It was appetite. And my understanding clicked too late, even as some darker part of me leaned into it, fascinated.

"Just a little taste," she murmured. "To seal

it."

Her teeth grazed my skin. The bond sang. And then she bit me.

Pain flared, brief and bright, then softened into something else entirely. It wasn't only pleasure. It was as if I could feel a deep, resonant pull, like a door opening inside me that I hadn't known was locked.

Lilith drank slowly, deliberately, but not greedily as she ground her hips against mine. Her mouth sealed over the wound at my throat, cool lips anchoring me as she took what she needed, one of my hands gripping her neck, the other threaded in her hair as I found myself rising to meet her with every stroke.

I felt it immediately, the way my power shifted to accommodate her, not draining but sharing, a current rerouted instead of diminished. The bond tightened again, humming low and eager, threading itself even deeper through muscle and bone until I could feel her heartbeat echoing faintly beneath my own.

She licked across the wound, sealing it, before she pulled back at last. Her eyes were dark, pupils blown wide, breath unsteady as she rode my cock. A thin line of my blood marked her mouth, vivid against her skin.

"There," she whispered, reverent now.

My hand came up without conscious thought, thumb brushing the corner of her mouth, smearing red. I grabbed her hips, guiding her, until she cried out, her muscles strangling my cock, and then I came again in near euphoria. But it didn't last long, as the need to sit up, as something in me demanded symmetry and completion, took over.

"You said equal," I said.

Lilith's smile was slow, unmistakably satisfied. She didn't argue. She tilted her head instead, exposing the pale curve of her throat, pulse steady and unguarded.

"Then take," she said softly.

I didn't hesitate. I flipped her onto her back, her hair splaying across the pillows.

I drew her closer, my mouth finding the place where her pulse lived. The taste was nothing like mine. Darker. Floral. Salt and night and something feral beneath it.

I lingered only a heartbeat before changing course, letting instinct pull me lower, away from her throat and down her body to where she opened wide for me, her scent mingling with mine, which made my mouth water.

I parted her with my tongue and licked and sucked until she came again, and when I bit, she gasped, fingers fisting in my hair, anchoring me as if she feared I might vanish if she let go.

I drank, not to consume, but to meet her there, to take her into myself the way she had taken me. The bond flared again, brighter this time, snapping into something that felt final.

Hell responded instantly. The flames in the room flared before going steady. Smoke stirred, and somewhere far below, the rivers hushed, their currents adjusting to a new gravity. The realm recognized what we had done and accepted it without protest.

When I finally raised back up, Lilith was trembling, her breath uneven, her grip still tight on my shoulders. I climbed back over her, and we stayed that way for a long moment, foreheads nearly touching, the bond between us warm and unmistakably alive.

"There," she said again, quieter now. "Now we're not just aligned."

I felt her inside me, a second presence woven cleanly through my power, not overriding it or diminishing it. We were now paired, shared as one.

"Equals," I said, the words heavier now.

Lilith met my gaze, something unreadable passing through her eyes. "Yes," she replied, "equals."

I told myself, foolishly, that this was completion. Not the beginning of something that would change the shape of my power forever.

CHAPTER FOUR

Lucifer

Hell was learning how to breathe. It didn't roar like I thought it would. It didn't burn endlessly or scream without pause. It exhaled, slowly, like something waking beneath a heavy weight, testing its own lungs.

I felt it each time I reshaped a part of it, the way stone loosened when I asked it to, the way fire calmed when it was given somewhere to go. Chaos wasn't the problem, but stagnation was. If I learned anything, it was that a realm that couldn't change and move would tear itself apart.

Mortals created the idea of a lake of fire down here, where souls burned eternally. There was no such thing, and I wasn't going to waste my time creating it. Hell didn't need flames to torment. It preferred memory and choices, and the slow grinding weight of consequence.

I stood barefoot on the upper terrace of the castle I'd built, the stone warm beneath my feet, watching the horizon settle into itself. Below, the land unfurled in deliberate lines, no longer a single endless pit but a body with systems, arteries, memory.

Rivers threaded through the lower levels of my Infernal Court. They weren't made of fire. They were made of black water so dense it swallowed reflection. Each river had its own temperament, its own cruelty.

Lethe ran thick and silent, its surface smooth as polished obsidian. One touch and memory unraveled. Love faded first. Even a touch of the fog could dissolve names. This one didn't steal everything at once. It erased in mercy. Slowly.

Acheron moved more heavily than the other rivers. It was sluggish, dense, and black as ink and wide as memory. A silver mist clung to its surface. It gathered the souls who had refused to choose, who had let life happen without conviction until choice was no longer theirs to make. They drowned without dying. Beneath the surface, they reached and clawed, tangling together in accusation and regret, desperate for the banks that never came. The current did not carry them forward. It held them. Suspended in consequence. Eternal in their refusal.

Styx coiled tight like a vow. Oily, unbreakable. Anything sworn in its presence binds itself tighter than iron. It remembered every promise ever made and punished those who forgot.

Phlegethon didn't burn. It scalded from within, like acid. The water slipped into your skin and turned regret into fever, forcing souls to relive the moment they knew better and chose wrong.

Cocytus was quieter. Thin. Bitter. Its waters tasted of salty tears, and the souls who drank from it could do nothing but weep for what they had lost, even if they could no longer remember what it was.

There were smaller tributaries, still unnamed and waiting to be finished as they shifted. But those streams whispered accusations and clung to souls as they took them down to the major rivers.

Along the banks, I placed newly formed demons, eager to please me. They stood waist-deep in the currents, hands outstretched, containing the souls that would otherwise tear themselves apart trying to escape. Others stood on the shores, long hooks in their hands, keeping them from escaping.

Boats followed. Bone-hulled, narrow, built for passage rather than comfort. Ferrymen came with them, creatures shaped for the work of crossing. They knew what to do without instruction. And somehow, so did I.

And that was the strangest part.

I didn't remember learning any of it. I only knew when something was wrong, when a slope needed gentling, when a river needed a bend, when a dead place needed a garden.

The Garden of the Forsaken grew where the land split too deeply to hold anything else. It wasn't burned or fertile, just… exhausted. The soil there had long forgotten things it no longer knew how to keep. I coaxed trees to grow, rising deformed, pale, and twisted. Their bark was veined with faint light that leaked instead of bled. Leaves crumbled to ash at the slightest touch. Flowers wilted before they ever had a chance to bloom.

I didn't know why I needed a garden that couldn't grow much of anything. I only knew that Hell felt wrong without it. It was a place for regret without redemption. Exile without spectacle.

Beyond it, I shaped the Crimson Verge. The land there glowed raw and red, pulsing like a wound that refused to close. Weapons grew from trees, from the earth, as naturally as roots. The ground drank blood and gave back rage sharpened into form. Souls crossed into it, believing they could fight their way out, believing struggle still meant something. From this place, they could see what they had lost. They could feel it, smell it, but they could never reach it.

Mercy and punishment braided so tightly I could no longer tell which hand I was using.

Further still, where sound itself had fractured, the Shattered Choir took shape. It was an amphitheater carved from ruin and memory. Broken columns. Melted instruments fused to stone and bone. Angels who had refused the war and fallen lingered there as residue rather than bodies, their music reduced to a hum that never resolved into song. There was never silence, but remembrance trapped mid-note. The air there vibrated with what might have been, with the cost of choosing nothing at all.

I never wanted a kingdom. I still didn't. But Hell had been given to me anyway, like a sentence delivered in silk, like an answer to a question I had never asked.

"You're trying to tame it," Lilith said behind me.

I didn't turn as I kept my focus. "I'm trying to make it hold," I said, reaching back for her hand. "If it fractures, it could devour itself."

She threaded her fingers through mine and came to stand beside me, close enough that I could smell the smoke under her floral scent and feel the cool of her skin against the warmth of the realm, a quiet contradiction. Lilith didn't carry Eden with her. Whatever softness she'd once been offered had been burned out by wandering, by salt air and sharp choices, by becoming something that didn't require permission to exist.

"Hell was never meant to hold," she said. "It was meant to punish."

"That's what they say about me now, too."

Her mouth curved, not quite a smile. Something like an agreement passed between us, unspoken and immediate. That was the thing I found myself returning to again and again, the way she understood without explanation. The way she didn't ask me to justify myself.

We were both bruised by the same hand—that counted for something.

Lilith leaned her forearms against the low balustrade and looked out over the forming realm. Below us, the fallen angels I'd left to their own devices were changing, stripping themselves down, and rebuilding themselves into demons shaped by hunger and adaptation rather than grace. They watched us the way animals watched fire, wary, reverent, waiting to see if it would warm them or burn them alive.

"They believe the story," she said quietly.

"Don't they always?" I asked.

The lie had spread faster than the Fall itself. Ambition. Pride. A hunger for the throne that had never been mine to take. I felt the shape of the accusations every time a soul looked at me with awe sharpened by fear.

Something about that story was wrong. I knew that in my bones, but I didn't know what was true, not entirely. The story they told didn't fit the hollow inside my chest. Ambition left a different wreckage. Pride didn't ache like grief.

Lilith tilted her head, studying me from the corner of her eye. "You don't sound angry."

"I was," I said. "At first."

"And now?"

I let my thoughts settle before I answered her. In the beginning, the anger had burned hot and bright and incandescent enough to threaten the fabric of this place. But anger required an object. A target. Something to strike against.

What I felt now was quieter.

"Now I've accepted the story," I said. "And I've decided to outlive it."

Lilith was quiet for a moment. She didn't seem surprised or even concerned. She just looked out at the realm, studying it.

Then her mouth curved slowly, the kind of smile that wasn't about warmth but recognition. "Yes," she said softly. "That's why this works. Fury tries to correct the story," she continued. "It demands to be rewritten."

Her eyes returned to mine. "But you?" she said. "You're building something that makes it irrelevant."

The words settled between us, heavier than maybe they should have been.

We hadn't named what we were doing, at least not formally, and not beyond the binding that tied our power together. We shared a bed, a life, but it wasn't devotion or love. It wasn't even a marriage.

It was survival.

And yet… Lilith moved through Hell as if it were already hers alone. She learned its systems quickly, its hierarchies, the way fear could be sharpened into obedience or dulled into chaos. Where I shaped the land, she shaped the rules. Where I created, she enforced.

We did not step on each other's work. And that alone felt miraculous.

"They're watching," she said after a moment.

"Who?"

She lifted a shoulder. "Does it matter? Everyone?"

It did, but I didn't respond. Heaven had not

looked away simply because I had fallen. If anything, the attention felt sharper now, like eyes pressed to glass, waiting for a mistake, a crack.

Lilith's gaze flicked upward, toward nothing I could see. Her jaw tightened, just slightly.

"They won't interfere," she added quickly. "Not as long as we're stable."

We—that word landed warm and dangerous in my chest.

I had not realized how alone I'd been until she arrived, how every decision echoed back at me unanswered. Hell demanded certainty, and certainty was difficult to maintain when you were the only one holding the line.

Lilith didn't question my right to the throne. She didn't flinch at my power. She didn't look at me as if I were something that had failed to become what it should have been.

She looked at me like an equal. That mattered more than I wanted to admit.

"Do you ever wonder," she said, carefully casual, "what would have happened if they'd listened instead?"

"To you?" I asked.

"To either of us," she corrected.

I frowned, the word snagging somewhere behind my ribs. "I don't know," I said. "I don't know that I trust the question."

Lilith smiled then, slow and knowing. "That's probably wise."

We stood in silence after that, the realm shifting and settling around us. Somewhere below, a river finished carving its path, and I raised my hands and with a motion it locked into place with a sound like distant thunder.

For the first time since the Fall, I felt something like equilibrium. Not peace, exactly, but a new balance of things. A sense that the weight on my shoulders was distributed, no longer mine alone to bear.

She was the one who decided to test that balance.

"Let's see if they believe in us," she said one night, sprawled across our bed like sin. "Not just fear. Belief. There's a difference."

"In what?" I asked. "Hell?"

"In us," she corrected. "In the bond. In the fact that this," she flicked two fingers toward the window where the horizon still glowed with half-made lands and half-finished punishments, "isn't a temper tantrum. It's a reign."

She called it a gathering, not a celebration. A celebration implied joy. A gathering implied intent. Word spread fast anyway.

By the time the first guests arrived, the great hall had remade itself around her vision.

Columns of obsidian rose from floor to ceiling, veined with a slow, molten red light. The ceiling opened onto a sky that wasn't a sky, just an endless dark streaked through with distant embers, like stars. The floor was polished black stone shot with red, reflective enough that every step looked like a footprint in fresh blood.

Lilith appeared at the top of the grand staircase in her signature red silk slip dress with a trailing hem, all exposed throat and lazy danger. The fabric caught the torchlight, so it looked less like clothing and more like blood that had decided to behave for the night. Her lips were the same color, and her smile was just as dangerous.

I stood beside her in black silk pants, with nothing on my chest but a leather harness that crossed from shoulder to hip, throwing daggers gleaming along its straps. The kind of thing you wore when you wanted everyone to remember you were armed long before you ever reached for a blade. An open black jacket hung loose off my frame, more suggestion than clothing.

The Fallen, now demons, came first. The ones who'd adapted quickly here. The ones who'd traded feathers for horns and halos for sharp teeth. Imps scurried at their heels, carrying trays laden with obsidian cups. The wine inside was the color of pomegranate seeds and something darker, thick enough to cling to the sides. Lilith had chosen it, and I was sure it wasn't just wine. Nothing here ever was.

The fallen who hadn't entirely chosen a new shape yet lingered near the walls, edges still too sharp, eyes still remembering other skies. Some wore remnants of their golden armor, and some nothing at all, too raw to care.

When Lilith decided to stay, she invited the Lilin with her. She claimed them as her creations, but I wasn't so sure. They were tall, long-limbed, and their movements were languid. Their hair spilled down their backs in dark rivers or pale sheets, threaded with fine chains that chimed softly when they shifted.

Gauze-thin fabrics clung to their hips and shoulders, barely there, revealing skin etched with faint sigils that glowed in the heat of the chamber. Their eyes were golden and glass-bright, reflecting the echo of every desire that had ever crossed the room.

Some knelt at the base of the dais. Others lounged against the black stone steps, as if the throne were simply another place to rest. They watched the court with small, knowing smiles, heads tilting in quiet unison whenever power shifted in the air.

They were not attendants. They were

temptation made flesh. They watched us the way they'd watched the throne, trying to decide if this was a court or a cage.

Lilith made sure it was both. She worked the room like a blade hidden in velvet. Laughing, touching, letting her cool fingers rest on forearms, shoulders, and mouths. She introduced me when it suited her, but everyone knew who I was.

"Your king," she'd purr, voice carrying just enough. "Angra Mainyu, if you're feeling modern. Lucifer, if you're feeling devout. Iblis, Samael, Shaitan, pick whichever story you crawled in with. Whatever name you use, he's the one who built this empire under your feet, every river, every torment, every inch of Hell you're so desperate to survive."

They bowed. Some out of fear. Some out of habit. A few out of something like respect. As they straightened, their attention flicked to her, gauging the angle of her mouth to decide how deeply they should have bowed.

She noticed. So did I.

Music grew out of the stones as the night lengthened. Not the fractured hum of the Shattered Choir, but something new, pulled from the throats and hands of those who'd once sung hymns and now had nothing sacred left to aim their voices at. Drums that sounded like distant thunder. Strings that wept and laughed in equal measure. It wasn't beautiful, but it was alive.

Games started in the corners. Wagers made on which soul would break first in friendly duels fought with weapons grown from the trees at the edges of the Crimson Verge and temporarily leashed to ritual instead of massacre. A circle formed where lesser demons showed off new forms, applauded or mocked depending on how cleverly they'd turned their old grace into new terror.

At the center of it all was our throne. I hadn't wanted it, but Lilith had insisted.

"Symbols matter," she'd said. "If they don't know where to look, they'll start trying to build their own altars. Trust me, you don't want that."

It was a seat carved from black stone threaded with veins of cooling magma, as if the heart of a volcano had been coaxed into furniture. It had widened for her ages ago. But tonight I'd taken a seat, and she slid into my lap. We weren't up on some elevated dais, not above them. We were just high enough that no one could pretend they didn't see us.

Every so often, a lesser demon or a newly-made lord would approach the base of the steps with some petition or gift. Most often, it was blood or information. Sometimes a captured oath. Lilith listened with her head tilted, eyes bright, sharp, making notes in her head that I couldn't see. I weighed what they brought with a glance and a question.

We didn't need to discuss most decisions. I could feel her judgment through the bond, the same way she could feel mine. When we did disagree, it was a subtle pressure in opposite directions, a moment of tension that resolved in the space of a heartbeat. Give this one lenience. Crush that one quickly. Let that rumor run. Cut this one off at the knees.

From the outside, it must have looked effortless.

At one point, a towering demon with molten cracks down his arms approached the base of the dais and dropped to one knee. "Sire," he said. "We heard you've bound your power together. We thought…"

He trailed off, glancing up through a curtain of singed hair.

"Thought what?" Lilith asked, amused.

"Thought it should be… marked," he said. "Witnessed."

The demon's voice barely finished echoing when I looked at him and stood. My movement alone quieted the chamber. Conversations faltered, laughter died, and the restless press of bodies stilled as Hell's attention shifted upward like iron filings toward a magnet.

I stepped to the edge of the platform.

"Careful," I said softly. "You're walking a very thin line between curiosity and insolence."

I stepped down, and the sound of my boots on the black stone echoed once, twice. By the third step, the room had gone completely silent.

He straightened instinctively as I approached, those molten seams along his arms flaring brighter in nervous reflex.

"You heard something?" I asked mildly.

"Yes, my king."

"And instead of trusting that I do as I please," I continued, my voice lowering just enough that the nearest creatures leaned in, "you thought you'd confirm it?"

His throat moved as he swallowed, and I stopped directly in front of him. Hell shifted with me, a subtle tightening in the air, like a hand closing around the room's spine.

"I rule this realm," I said softly. "If I bind my power to another, it is not because I must." I leaned closer. "It is because I choose."

The demon dropped fully to both knees before I even lifted a finger, his hands braced against the stone as pressure settled into his bones. He bowed his head lower as the heat in the room changed.

The torches all flared to attention. It wasn't just fire, though. I let the pressure settle into bone and reminded every creature present exactly whose realm they were standing in.

"Does that answer satisfy you?" I asked the room at large.

No one spoke.

Lilith rose and came down to stand beside me, her hand sliding lightly along my arm. But my gaze remained on the kneeling demon as his head went to the ground.

She leaned toward my ear, "Let's show them," she murmured.

Only then did I turn my head. She was watching me, her eyes gleaming.

I could have refused and reminded them all that I didn't respond to speculation.

I turned back to the room, "You want it witnessed?" I asked.

My voice darkened and carried without effort, threading through the hall until even the creatures at the far arches lifted their heads.

"Then watch."

Power answered the command before I consciously reached for it. The fires running through the floor flared, bright veins of molten light streaking outward from the throne. Somewhere deep beneath the palace, the wild rivers roared, and the stone itself shifted, like a massive creature stretching awake.

A thousand demons lowered their heads at once. The kneeling one remained prostrate on the floor. I let the power build just long enough for every soul in the chamber to feel it pressing against their ribs. Then I drew it back, folding it inward again like a blade sliding into its sheath.

Silence followed.

I held out my hand. Lilith took it, her cool fingers wrapping around my wrist. Her nails lengthened, sharpening just enough to break skin. A thin line of dark blood welled up where she dragged them across my palm.

There was no sound as she lifted my hand to her mouth and sank her teeth in, just enough to taste. The bond flared, hot and bright, tightening around our joined power until it was hard to tell where mine stopped, and hers began.

Then she offered me her wrist. Her pulse beat there, sluggish and methodical. Her skin was pale, her veins red—the promise of something ancient under the surface.

I bit, and the flavor of her hit my tongue like old salt and night wind, like the Red Sea she'd found after Eden. The bond shuddered, then settled, our shared power knitting tighter, cleaner.

Lilith's breath left her in a soft laugh.

Before the moment could fade, I caught her hand again and pressed our wounded palms together, grinding the blood between them until it coated both our skin. Then I lifted our joined hands high above us. The smears of crimson caught the firelight, bright as a banner.

For a long moment, no one in the throne room moved. Demons bowed their heads. Succubi stilled. The Lilin lowered their eyes. Even the restless fires in the floor seemed to quiet.

I tilted my head slightly and smirked. "Witnessed enough?" I asked.

And Hell did.

Wickedness loved a show. The demons roared. Some in delight, some in vicious approval, all of them accepting that this was how Hell was ruled now. Not by a single furious exile, but by two creatures who'd refused to stay where they were put and found each other in the fallout.

The music started up again as the revel came back to life. For a moment, I let myself feel it. Not just the dominance. The… companionship. The sense that if I fell, someone would be dragged down with me, not out of pity but out of sheer, stubborn tether.

We left the throne later, when the gathering had turned messy and soft around the edges. Lilith led me down into the crowd, let the music swallow us. We danced, if you could call it that. Bodies pressed in around us, heat and cold and hunger. She laughed against my mouth, teeth grazing my lower lip, eyes bright with genuine thrill.

"This is ours," she said breathlessly into my ear as I used my hand to give her pleasure. "We built this."

For once, I didn't argue. For once, I believed her. And if there was a flaw in it, I didn't see it, couldn't see it. If there was a cost, it hadn't been named.

Later, when the hall had emptied into whispers and ash, we took a succubus whom Lilith had taken a liking to back to our rooms. It was easy, wicked fun, the kind of distraction Hell expected from its rulers. When it was over, she slept tangled at the foot of our bed, wings slack, hair a dark spill across the sheets. Lilith dozed beside me, one cool arm thrown over my stomach like she meant to claim even my dreams.

But a while later, I slipped free and stepped out onto the balcony, leaving the scent of sex and wine and sin behind me. Night pressed close around the castle, lit from below by the slow glow of magma veins running through the land and the steady pulse of the rivers.

The air rolled up from the chasms below, hot and metallic, carrying the distant roar of things that had never learned to be quiet.

Someone had left a small bundle of Ma beside the wine.

I took one between my fingers. The dried herb had been wrapped tightly in a thin strip of reed, twisted at one end so it would burn slowly. I leaned toward the torch fixed in the wall and held the tip to the flame until it caught, the end glowing dull orange.

Smoke curled upward at once. I drew in slowly. The taste was bitter and green, ancient as the earth itself, and the smoke spread warm through my chest before spilling back out into the dark.

Below me, Hell moved and groaned and shifted. I leaned my forearms on the stone railing and watched Acheron carve its dark path as Lethe slid quietly, like a knife, through memory.

I told myself that this, at least, was real. That this alliance, this shared rage, this understanding forged from rejection and loss and sealed in blood before all of Hell, was solid. That I wasn't wrong to trust her.

Hell breathed beneath my feet, warm and steady, and for a moment, I let myself believe it would hold.

CHAPTER FIVE

Lucifer

I started to rise from the bed, the need sharp and insistent, but Lilith shifted behind me before I could sit up. I hadn't planned to take her with me or explain why. But her fingers were insistent as they slid down my chest, not exploratory or gentle, just certain, like she already knew exactly how to convince me to forget everything.

"Where are you going?" she asked, her voice low and smooth, the way predators keep their prey calm.

I simply said, "There are parts of Hell that don't need an entourage."

She didn't answer right away. Her hand slid lower, down my stomach, pressure increasing just enough to make it a choice to move instead of an instinct. She wrapped her fingers around me and began to stroke. The bond stirred, attentive, leaning toward her touch as if it recognized the danger before I did.

"You're restless," she murmured, a dangerous softness in her voice. "That usually means something needs attention."

Her thumb traced once around my crown, slow and deliberate, like she was testing my response. "Whatever you're chasing can wait. I'm right here."

When I didn't reach for her, she withdrew her hand and inclined her head, granting permission. And maybe that was when my warning bells should've gone off. But they didn't. I just climbed out of bed and left as quickly as I could.

At the last bend of Acheron, the Riverlands, I stepped off Aluma's boat, and the land split open into the Shattered Choir. I passed through its thin, reverent hum. The sound clung to the air like a broken hymn that refused to die.

I skimmed the edge of the Crimson Verge just as a battle began to gather, steel ringing in the distance, the first cries sharp against the dark. I didn't intervene. I didn't announce myself.

By the time I crested the ridge, the withered great tree loomed ahead, its hollowed trunk yawning wide like a mouth waiting to swallow confession—the entrance to the Garden of the Forsaken.

And still. Still, I had to enter through its throat. Thousands of years, and I hadn't changed that. I'd reshaped rivers and lands to my will. I'd made the throne rise and harden into something inevitable.

But the Garden? I still had to slip inside it like a secret. Through the mouth of a dead tree. Through splintered bark and shadow, as if I were sneaking into something outlawed instead of ruling the realm that surrounded it.

I'd meant to change that. Meant to split the sky above it, carve a gate worthy of a king, and meant to make my entrance unmistakable. Instead, I stood at the edge of the maw, hesitating.

A king shouldn't have to bow his head to enter anything. And yet, every time, I did. Willingly. It waited below, pale and stubborn against the ruin. And I still hadn't claimed it the way I'd claimed everything else.

The air changed the moment I crossed into it, not cooler, but quieter. Sound behaved differently. It softened. Even my footsteps felt like an intrusion.

The Garden grew in defiance of its surroundings, pale and stubborn. Trees twisted upward, their bark always split with faint veins of strange gold light that leaked instead of bled. I caught a leaf drifting slowly as it crumbled in my hand to nothing.

I told myself this place was for them. For the angels who'd fallen and broken on impact. For the ones who hadn't survived the descent intact, who'd become something else entirely or nothing at all. A place for what Heaven had discarded without ceremony.

That was the explanation I gave Hell, but it wasn't the truth. The truth was simpler. I was the only one who came here. No one followed me or stood guard here. I hadn't commanded it, but they knew to stay away.

After I entered, I walked for hours without meaning to measure them. Time thinned in this place. It didn't move the way it did elsewhere. It pooled. It lingered.

The Garden didn't resist me. Dark branches curved overhead like the ribs of something vast and long-dead, enclosing without quite trapping. Veins of strange gold light ran through the bark, pulsing faintly beneath the surface.

Which was curious. Because I hadn't willed it to.

I hadn't always had a castle. There had been a time, long before, when this was where I slept, hidden in a grotto deep in the Garden.

It revealed itself gradually, half-swallowed by twisting roots and hanging black vines that seemed to part only for me. The entrance was narrow, the stone inside smooth from age and proximity. I stepped into it without hesitation.

This had been my refuge once. My exile within exile, away from everything else.

For the first thousand years, I'd slept here against the cold wall, wings wrapped around myself like they could replace what I'd lost. I had refused the half-made throne and refused the title. Refused the shape of the thing they said I'd become.

I had come here instead, night after night, as though proximity to something only half growing might keep me from unraveling entirely. The wall was still there. The hollow in the stone where my back had pressed was still faintly visible.

And in the corner, half-covered in dust and brittle leaves, lay a small pile of fabric and metal. My old clothes were little more than tattered remnants, stiff with time, and still embedded with ash in the weave. My golden armor was now broken and tarnished. I didn't remember leaving them here. I didn't remember taking them off or ever looking for them. But something in me hitched as I stepped closer.

I knelt and reached out, brushing my fingers over the cloth. The moment I lifted it, something small and smooth slipped free and struck the ground with a muted sound.

A stone. It was unremarkable at first glance. Pale. Rounded. Worn smooth by touch or time. It shouldn't have meant anything. I picked it up, and the world narrowed. It fit perfectly in my palm. It was warm. But it wasn't from the Garden or Hell. It was from… Heaven, from memory. I knew that instinctively.

I stared at it, searching for recognition that never came. I had no recollection of carrying it. No memory of why it would have been in my pocket the day I fell. And yet the weight of it pressed into me like something precious. Like something chosen. A remembrance, like something I had once refused to let go.

The Garden felt closer suddenly. Quieter. As if it, too, was waiting for me to remember.

I left the grotto and walked deeper between the trees, to the hollow near the center where the ground dipped naturally, where my own version of the Tree of Knowledge had grown twisted and now was barren. I knelt and pressed my palm to the soil. It didn't respond to my will the way the rest of the realm did. It didn't reshape itself or warm beneath my touch.

It simply waited.

I dug into the soil with my hands. The earth

parted easily, welcoming, as if it recognized what I was offering. I placed the stone carefully into the hollow and covered it again, pressing the dirt flat with deliberate care.

The moment my hands stilled, something in me broke. Grief surged up without warning, sharp and disorienting, stealing the breath from my lungs. It wasn't sorrow with a shape or a story. It wasn't even a memory. It was just… loss, vast and immediate, like I'd set something down that had mattered more than anything and realized too late there was no way to reach for it again.

My chest ached with that feeling of loss, a hollow pressure that didn't belong to any wound I could name. I pressed my fist to the earth, harder this time, trying to pull something from the rock, from the ground, from… anything, as if it might explain itself, as if it might give something back.

Nothing came.

I bowed my head, shoulders curling inward despite myself, breath catching on something dangerously close to a sob. Panic flashed hot through the grief, not because of what I felt, but because of where I was feeling it.

I was the ruler of Hell. I couldn't afford to be anything soft, anything breakable. Not here. Not where the realm listened, and the dead always watched, and even silence could become rumor.

There was never anyone here but me. No one ever followed me here. But I forced my spine straight, my eyes flicking to the trees as if they might be hiding witnesses. My hand went to my throat on instinct, as if I could physically shove the sound back down before it escaped.

I hated the weakness of it. I hated that the feeling had no cause I could name, no memory to justify its weight. I hated most of all that it wasn't rage, because rage I understood. Rage was useful. Grief was a door left open.

I drew a slow breath through my nose and held it until the tremor in my chest quieted. Until my face went still. Until the mask fit again. Only then did I look back down at the place I'd buried the stone, and realized I felt... fear.

"I don't understand," I whispered to the soil, but the Garden remained still.

The grief didn't ease, but it settled, sinking deeper, embedding itself somewhere in my chest like it meant to stay. And somehow, impossibly, I knew this wasn't the first time I'd felt it. It was just the first time I'd noticed.

The strange golden light in the bark of the surrounding trees pulsed once, faint and bright, then stilled again. For a heartbeat, the knowing brushed close. *Of course,* my mind supplied. *Of course it was because—*

But the thought collapsed the moment I reached for it, dissolving before it could take shape. Whatever it was slipped away, leaving only the ache behind, heavier for having almost remembered.

I returned the next day. And the day after that. The Garden drew me back with a persistence that bordered on need and desperation. I walked its paths when the rest of Hell grew too loud, too obedient, too heavy with expectation. I knelt by the place where I'd buried the stone and spoke to it, as if it were an old friend, said words I didn't remember learning, prayers without gods to hear them.

After that, I had a mission. I began bringing things with me. Seeds at first. Then saplings. I crossed into Earth's realm alone, unannounced, choosing plants that had survived neglect, that had grown crooked and stubborn in poor soil. I carried them back into Hell cupped in my hands like offerings. For a few days, sometimes weeks, they'd hold. Then they'd wither—every damn time. I hated the Garden for it. I hated myself more.

I kept coming back, but I didn't notice her. That was the unsettling part. It wasn't until the third time I felt it that I realized there was the faintest pressure at the edge of my awareness. Not the weight of the bond, but something adjacent to it, like attention, careful and measured. And watching.

I chose not to confront her. I finished tending the sapling I already knew wouldn't last, then rose and left the Garden without looking back.

That night back at the castle, Lilith found me. She didn't throw accusations. She didn't even question. She came to me with softness instead, cool hands sliding around my shoulders from behind, her touch settling like frost against warm stone. Her smile asked for nothing and offered everything.

"You've been distant," she murmured, fingers tracing slow patterns across my chest. "You don't have to carry all of this alone."

The bond leaned eagerly into her touch. Familiar. Hungry. Sometimes I wondered if it was too familiar.

I closed my eyes, trying to listen past the sensation, past the quiet pull in my veins that always urged me to lean back into her. Instead, I spoke the truth that had been gnawing at me.

"I don't know what's happening there," I said. "The Garden. It won't accept anything I bring to it."

Lilith hummed softly, thoughtful. "Maybe

it isn't meant to."

"Why does it feel like it is?"

She moved closer, pressing against my back, her voice lowering as if the walls themselves might overhear. "Does it… remind you of something?"

The question slid into place too neatly. My eyes opened.

"No." I turned just enough to look at her. Held her gaze without blinking. "If you're trying to make me say Eden, don't."

The word felt ornamental. Decorative. I had rarely set foot there. It had never belonged to me. "It's a Garden," I said evenly. "That's all."

I looked away then. My fingers curled at my side before I could stop them. Bone grinding faintly in the joints. An old instinct stirring under my skin. A reflex that had once ended arguments by snapping spines instead of finishing sentences.

I forced my hand still. Lilith's attention dropped to it immediately.

She studied my face, searching. Waiting. "Are you sure?" she asked gently. "Because I think you want it to. I think you're looking for something you lost."

Her words should've comforted me. They didn't. They felt like bait drifting across dark water.

I stepped forward just enough to slip from her arms. The bond tightened in protest, a hot thread pulling between us.

"You've been following me," I said quietly.

Lilith didn't deny it. "I worried," she replied. "That's all."

Something in me snapped tight. Before I could think better of it, I turned and caught her wrist, not gently. My fingers closed around the slender bones there, pinning her arm between us. The motion was fast enough that the air shifted with it, a subtle tremor running through the chamber as if Hell itself had flinched.

Lilith didn't gasp. She didn't pull away. Her eyes lifted to mine, cool and unreadable.

I was aware, distantly, of how little pressure it would take to break what I was holding. A flick. A twist. The knowledge pulsed through me, old and intimate.

My grip tightened. Just enough to remind her.

"Don't," I said, voice low and rough.

The bond flared hot between us, not pleased with the tension. It wanted me to soften. To lean in. I didn't.

For a heartbeat, the darker part of me pressed forward — the part that had learned that dominance was clearer than doubt. I could have forced her to her knees. I could have bent her until the truth fell out of her mouth in pieces.

Instead, I exhaled, slowly, deliberately. My thumb shifted against her pulse, feeling how steady it was. She wasn't afraid. She was watching me. Measuring. That realization cooled me faster than reason. I loosened my grip just enough that it wasn't a threat anymore.

"If you follow me again," I said quietly, "you'll tell me first."

Lilith's lips curved faintly. "I would never hide from you," she said.

Which wasn't the same thing at all.

I released her wrist. I only nodded once, because nodding was easier than admitting how exposed I felt. The air between us settled. But the violence didn't disappear. It simply folded back inside me.

She tried again and took my hand, fingers cool and sure, and drew me back toward our rooms as if the conversation had already ended. I followed as if this were the natural end to unease.

Inside, I pressed her against the familiar stone and kissed her, slower this time. She dragged me to the bed, coaxing rather than asking. It was practiced. Comfortable. A dance we'd done thousands of times. The kind of intimacy that required nothing difficult from either of us.

I went through the motions because it was easier than refusing. Because stillness could be mistaken for consent, and distance could be hidden beneath routine. I kept my face composed, my thoughts carefully elsewhere, giving her nothing she could trace back to the Garden or the grief or the thing she was so intent on drawing out of me.

When it was over, she rested against me like she'd settled something, and I stared up at the ceiling and waited for the bond to tell me I'd chosen right. It didn't.

The next morning, when I rose, she did too. I went down the stairs and didn't need to look back to know she'd followed. I could feel it in the bond, the warm pressure of her attention tightening like a hand around my wrist.

I stopped abruptly on the last step. "Don't," I said without turning.

Lilith's laugh was quiet, almost fond. "Don't what?"

"Don't come."

She appeared beside me anyway, already dressed in tight black leathers and boots as if she'd anticipated the refusal. Her eyes glittered with something too sharp for sleep. "You keep going alone," she said. "That's not what equals do."

"It's not about equals."

"It's about secrets," she corrected, sweetly. "And you don't get to have them from me."

The bond hummed at that, eager, persuasive, as if it wanted to agree with her on my behalf.

I clenched my jaw and started walking again. Lilith fell into step as if it were her right.

The journey to the Garden of the Forsaken took us beyond the last bend of Acheron into the Riverlands, where the air softened, and heat withdrew into the earth. The closer we got, the quieter the realm became.

There wasn't any screaming this far out, and the sound once again thinned until even our footsteps seemed too loud. Lilith didn't seem to notice, or maybe she did and enjoyed it.

"So this is your little shrine," she said, gaze sweeping the withered expanse of trees. "I thought it'd be… prettier."

I didn't answer. I just went forward and crawled through the great maw opening and waited for her.

The hollow inside smelled of sour sap and old earth that had never known fire. The bark curved around me like ribs, shielding, hiding, as if the Garden itself had decided where I should stand. I climbed out but stayed still, breath slow, listening to the way the place held its silence.

When she started to crawl through, I felt the change before she emerged. The Garden shifted. It wasn't visible, but I felt it the way you feel a room turn cold when someone unwelcome steps inside. A subtle withdrawal. A recoil.

The faint golden veins in the bark dimmed, as if the trees had drawn their light inward. Leaves that had drifted lazily like ash moments before stilled midair, then sank too quickly, crumbling before they should have.

I was sure the Garden knew the difference between us. It didn't want her. And that should have satisfied me. Instead, doubt pressed in.

Was it her? Was it what she was, the hunger in her blood, the cold intelligence that never truly rested?

Or was it me? Had I carried something into this place the first time I entered it, something fractured, something unfinished, that it had been reacting to all along?

Or worse—was it both of us? Two forces braided too tightly together, confusing whatever this place had been before I found it. Was the Garden recoiling from her presence… or from the bond between us?

Something in my chest squeezed again, that same tension as before. Only this time it wasn't grief. It was suspicion. A warning that didn't point outward. It pointed inward.

I waited for her to come through, to understand what the Garden already seemed to know. I didn't move. Instead, I watched through the split in the trunk as Lilith stepped closer, her presence sharp against the hush, her footsteps too loud in a place that preferred reverence.

She dusted herself off and walked forward, hands clasped behind her back, inspecting the place like it was an imperfect room in a house she'd purchased.

"Is this where you go to pretend you're still… what?" she asked, glancing back at me with a lazy smile. "Soft?"

My throat went tight. I stepped in front of her before she could drift closer to the center.

"Don't," I said, sharper this time.

Her brow lifted. "Don't touch your sacred dirt?"

"It's not—" I stopped, because I didn't have a word that didn't sound ridiculous. I didn't have a reason that didn't sound like longing. And my longing was one thing I refused to hand her.

Lilith's eyes narrowed, amused. "You're acting like it's alive."

"It is," I said before I could stop myself.

The Garden held its breath around us.

Lilith's smile widened, pleased in the way predators get pleased when they feel a nerve.

"Does it speak to you?" she asked, voice dipping into softness. "Does it tell you things?"

My skin prickled. "No."

She stepped closer anyway, the cool of her presence brushing the air. The bond leaned forward, eager, too eager, like it wanted to fold me back into her before I could think.

Something hot and immediate surged up my spine. "I'm building a realm," I said, the words coming out sharper than I intended. "That's all."

The air around us shifted with it. A low tremor ran through the roots beneath our feet, fine cracks splintering through the stone at the base of the withered tree.

"That's all," I repeated, more quietly this time, which was worse.

The golden veins in the bark flickered, then flared in answer to the heat bleeding off me. I stepped closer to her, not enough to touch, but enough that the space between us felt charged. My jaw tightened.

Lilith tilted her head. "Are you sure?"

The Garden's light dimmed again, almost imperceptibly, like it was flinching. I felt it again. The recoil. The refusal. And it hit me like a blade sliding between ribs.

It wasn't rejecting me. It was rejecting her.

The ground answered first. Dead vines, blackened and brittle, slithered down from the trees into sudden, angry knots. They lashed, sliding across the earth with a purpose that wasn't hunger so much as repulsion.

They went for her ankles, trying to snare her and drag her back out. One coil snapped tight, yanking hard enough that Lilith had to shift her weight to keep her footing. Another struck across her boot like a whip.

This place wanted her gone.

Lilith glanced down, startled now, the amusement cracking at the edges. "Well," she breathed, as if offended by the audacity.

I moved without thinking. I caught her by the elbows, steadying her as I kicked the vines away, hard, scattering brittle coils and snapping tendrils before they could catch again. The ends twitched like severed nerves, still reaching, still trying to drive her back.

The trees pulsed faintly, their veins of light tightening inward, as if the Garden itself was holding its breath in disgust.

Lilith's eyes flicked to mine, sharp and bright. "It hates me," she said, like she couldn't decide whether to laugh or take it personally.

I stared at the ruined vines in the dirt, at the way the Garden had reacted to her like an immune response.

"Leave," I said, the word low and flat.

Lilith's smile returned, slower this time, but it didn't reach her eyes. "Is that what *you* want," she murmured, "or is that what *it* wants?"

I didn't answer. Because for the first time, I couldn't tell if the Garden was protecting me, or warning me about something I'd already let too close.

She glanced around, her eyes briefly flicking to me, as if she could sense the shift even if she didn't understand it.

Her mouth twitched, irritation flashing beneath the amusement. "Lucy? What exactly is this place?"

I stared at her. At the ease with which she'd mocked it, at the hunger behind her curiosity, at the way her softness always arrived right before a question she needed answered.

My voice came out low. Controlled. "It's mine."

Something flickered in her gaze, fast and unreadable. Then she smiled again, too smooth, too practiced, her hips swaying as she walked up to me, her fingers foxtrotting along my chest.

"Then let me in," she whispered.

The bond tightened, urging me toward her with a heat that felt less like want and more like momentum. It was a habit, a path I'd walked often enough that my body knew it before my mind could object.

I caught her wrist before she could pull me closer. It wasn't rough or gentle, but firm enough to stop the dance. Lilith glanced down at my hand, then back up at me, her amusement sharpening into something colder.

"You're hesitating," she said softly. "You never hesitate with me."

I released her wrist and stepped back, breaking the pull. The Garden exhaled, light returning to the trees in a faint, relieved pulse.

Lilith watched it happen. Watched me notice. And in that small silence, something in me finally rearranged itself. This had never been what I'd told myself it was. It hadn't been two rejected, lonely people finding balance in each other's ruin. It hadn't even been understanding. And it certainly hadn't been equals.

This had all been about leverage. She didn't want a partnership. She didn't want to rule beside me as an equal force. She'd wanted proximity, the kind that let her feel what I felt and hear what I didn't say. She'd wanted a place inside my power where she could listen for something. She wanted something from me. I just didn't know what yet.

"I'm thinking," I replied.

Lilith's gaze stayed on me, steady and intent, like she wasn't watching my face so much as waiting for something beneath it to twitch.

"About the Garden?" she prompted, casual enough to pass for interest. "About the way you keep trying to make something dead behave like it's… meant for life?"

I didn't answer. I didn't give her anything to hold on to.

But she stepped closer anyway, voice dropping into that coaxing softness she used when she wanted the truth from a damned soul without having to ask for it outright. "Are you sure you're not… reaching for something?"

That… hit differently because she'd already asked. Not with those words, but the point underneath hadn't changed.

Why did she need to know so badly? It didn't feel like just curiosity. She was looking for something, wanted something from me, and this felt like a checkpoint, like she needed something to report back to someone, whether I'd crossed it.

My stomach twisted hard with a sudden, violent déjà vu, as if my body recognized the truth before my mind could form it. For a heartbeat, I tasted it, the shape of the answer.

Yes.

I knew it in my bones. That was exactly what I was doing. But in the same instant, something colder rose up and locked into place. It wasn't fear or even anger, but a quiet instinct, ancient and absolute.

Don't tell her.

I looked at Lilith and felt distaste flare, clean and sharp. Not because she'd asked me, but because she'd asked again.

"No," I said, voice flat enough to make it boring. "Why would I want to remember anything from Heaven?"

Her eyes searched mine, not for emotion, but for leakage. For the seam where the lie might split. Then her expression softened into satisfaction, the way a hand relaxes after it tightens around a leash.

"Good," she said lightly, and her fingers brushed mine, grounding, reassuring, almost tender. Like she'd just guided me back onto the right path.

So I adjusted my face. Let my shoulders loosen. I stepped back into her space and gave her a smile I didn't feel and placed my hand on the small of her back, the kind of thing that passed for trust if you didn't look too closely.

"Let's go back home," I said quietly.

The bond warmed at my lies, mistaking

performance for trust. Her eyes brightened, satisfied, and she reached for me as if she'd steadied something that had almost tipped.

I let her. Not because I believed her. But because from that moment on, I understood I couldn't afford to let her know that I didn't.

But that night, she went to a party, and I returned to the Garden alone. I knelt where the stone lay buried and pressed my forehead to the soil, breathing in the quiet.

"I don't know what I'm doing wrong," I whispered.

The Garden didn't answer. But it didn't reject me either.

I went there more often after that, whenever Lilith had something else to do. I stopped bringing plants. I stopped trying to make it live. I just sat beneath the twisted Tree of Knowledge like I was communing with its ruined nature, or maybe just my own.

And every time Lilith touched me after, every time she tried to draw me back into her seduction and distraction, I felt the distance between us grow clearer. She was trying to pull something out of me. I didn't know what it was yet. But one thing had become crystal clear—Lilith wasn't afraid of the Garden. She was afraid of what it might reveal.

CHAPTER SIX

Lucifer

We stepped onto Earth in the middle of a prayer.

The air here was different, scrubbed sharp by smoke and incense from the fire altars below. White stone buildings climbed the hill in ordered layers, courtyards wrapped around flames that never went out. Priests moved between them with covered mouths so their breath wouldn't touch what they called holy.

They called Him Ahura Mazda in this empire. Wise Lord. They called me Angra Mainyu. The Destructive Spirit. The Adversary. Neat little labels so they didn't have to look too closely at who had written the story.

My boots hit packed earth at the edge of the road. The sword strapped across my back settled into place with a familiar weight. Sariel stepped out beside me, cloak knocking the dust as he shifted, his own blade visible over his shoulder so no one could pretend they'd missed the message.

"The villa's just beyond that rise," he said quietly, nodding toward a walled compound overlooking the city. "Servants have cleared the grounds."

Of course, they had. When you invite the devil, you make sure there are no witnesses who'll gossip to the wrong altar.

Behind us, the rest of the entourage she had insisted on bringing spilled through the tear, shadows stepping into the sun. Fallen angels. Lesser demons. Creatures who knew how to keep their eyes down and their ears open.

And Lilith.

She didn't wear the veil the way local women did. She wore it like an accessory, linen draped loosely, not hiding a thing. Halfway down the slope, she reached up and tugged the thin fabric free, letting it fall around her shoulders. The gesture bared her throat and, when she smiled, the clean white points of her fangs.

A priest near the closest fire temple stuttered mid-chant.

Lilith had a new plaything, Vespera. She walked at her side, horns uncovered, black and gleaming like polished obsidian. People's gazes snagged on her and skittered away again. Nephilim was the rumor, or something worse. No one had asked her outright. No one wanted the answer.

Lilith left her behind and caught up to me easily and slipped her arm through mine as we took the road down toward the villa, her veil now trailing like a small surrender flag.

"You do enjoy being stared at," I murmured.

"Fear behaves better when it's impressed." Her lips curved, a slow, wicked thing. "Wasn't it you who taught me that?"

I glanced down at her, at the way she'd bared her fangs while taking my arm, daring the pious to look away.

"You wear the role well," I said. "They'll be talking about you for years."

She preened a little at that, looking pleased. Vespera had caught up with us, and her mouth ticked up on one side, a private echo of the same satisfaction.

That was new, the way Vespera mirrored her, the way her attention sat on Lilith first and everyone else second. What had started as a simple indulgence had become… consistent and intentional.

The last few times she'd shared our bed, they'd spent more of it wrapped in each other, laughter and low conspiracies threaded between pleasure, half their words in a language of glances I wasn't fluent in.

Lilith had chosen to give her rooms in my castle. Rooms, plural. That was permanence, not novelty. She was building something. Around herself. Inside my walls.

We reached the gates of the merchant's villa. Servants threw them open the moment they saw us, dropping into bows that were a little too deep, a little too fast. The courtyard inside had been scrubbed bare of leaves, dust, and anyone who might repeat what they heard.

The merchant waited near the central fountain, rings heavy on his fingers, robe embroidered with scenes of winged figures spreading blessing and order. His eyes punched straight past the entourage to me, then to Lilith, then to the sharp gleam of Vespera's horns.

He folded to one knee before his body finished deciding.

"Angra Mainyu," he said, voice shaking. "Lord of Chaos. Destruc—"

"That's enough," I cut in. "You wanted a bargain. Say what you want."

He swallowed. "My sons," he said hoarsely. "My house. I want them protected. From plague. From famine. From those who would see us ruined. If I give what is mine to give—"

"What you have," I said, "is always yours to give. That's the only thing that makes this a bargain instead of theft."

His gaze flicked to the stone under his hands, then up to the distant glimpse of a fire altar beyond the wall. "Ahura Mazda cares for those who are righteous," he said carefully. "This is only to… secure myself against my own failures."

So he wanted me to catch what his god missed. The irony didn't bother him as much as it should have.

Lilith drifted a fraction closer, veil swaying. To him, it would feel like being inspected by a queen. She smiled just enough to show a hint of fang.

"Righteousness is… flexible," she said lightly. "Intention matters less than outcome. You want your line to continue. You want your wealth to remain. You're honest about it. That's almost… admirable."

Almost.

He looked at her the way men look at pretty things that could also end them.

We discussed terms. I walked him through the cost, no theatrics, no sudden raised voice, just calm inevitability of what it would take, what he'd owe—his soul. The point was years from now, when he'd realize how narrow the path he'd chosen really was.

He hesitated in all the expected places. He agreed anyway. Greed and fear of loss always weighed more heavily than the fear of damnation.

Sariel unrolled the contract as I took the merchant's hand before he could reconsider. His pulse fluttered against my thumb, mortal and fragile.

A slow exhale of shadow spilled from my skin and condensed into metal, the blade forming like a thought I'd already decided to act on.

"You understand the cost," I said.

He nodded.

I didn't hesitate. I drew the edge slowly across his palm, not deep enough to maim, just deep enough to make the lesson linger. Just enough to make him hiss and look at me like I had already stolen something that mattered. Blood welled instantly, dark and bright in the torchlight.

I turned his hand upward and pressed my thumb into the wound, widening it slightly, making sure it would scar.

"Good," I murmured. "It should hurt."

"Hold," I said.

He did. Trembling, but he did.

Sariel smoothed the parchment against the low stone table in the center of the courtyard. To us, this was all routine. But to the merchant, it might as well have been an altar. The script that crawled across the page was not in any language the man recognized, with curves and hooks that refused to sit still if you looked at them too long.

Lilith had stepped closer without him noticing, veil loose, fangs hidden now, eyes bright. "You asked for this, remember," her voice deceptively gentle at his shoulder.

He glanced at her as if that would save him. It did not.

Sariel tapped the bottom of the page. "Here," he said.

I tilted the merchant's wrist and let the blood run. It hit the parchment, and the ink twitched, lines bending to meet it like thirsty roots. The symbols drank him in, greedily, curling around the drops as if they had been waiting for this particular taste.

The merchant stared, breath coming too fast. "What does it say?" he whispered.

"It says you wanted your sons to live long enough to inherit everything you are afraid to lose," I replied. "And it says you are willing to let something else die for that."

His throat bobbed. "What dies?"

"You," I said. "Eventually. That was always true. I am only adjusting the timing."

Behind him, Vespera watched with her head slightly tipped, as if she were studying technique rather than morality. Her gaze followed the way the ink locked around each drop of blood, how the parchment darkened for a heartbeat and then went pale again, the pact sinking out of sight.

Sariel wiped the blade clean with a strip of cloth, efficient, unbothered. He rerolled the contract, the edges now stained the faintest reddish brown.

"It is done," I said.

The merchant pulled his hand back and cradled it against his chest, already trying to convince himself the cut was the worst of it.

"Keep it wrapped for a day," Lilith added, as if she were giving him some domestic kindness. "You don't want it getting infected."

He nodded too eagerly, grateful for anything that sounded like care. And our bond hummed, smug and synchronized, a shared current of satisfaction at how cleanly we'd played our parts.

I watched him, watched the way relief tried to settle on his shoulders and couldn't quite find purchase. Another soul who had talked himself into believing the cost was acceptable.

"You got what you asked for," I reminded him, letting just a fraction of heat bleed into my eyes. "Don't pretend you were tricked."

His gaze jerked up to mine, stunned, as if I

had read a thought he had not dared to form fully yet. I had. They all had the same thoughts in the end.

When it was done, he pressed his forehead to the stone again, fingers digging into the cracks like they could hold him in place.

"Rise," I said. "Live the life you've purchased. I'll come collect when it ends."

He flinched like I'd already touched him, and we left him there.

Back in the street, the city moved around us in carefully orchestrated denial. No one stared directly. No one ran. That was the thing about a monotheistic empire, their fear had rules.

Sariel took point as we headed back toward the rise, cloak sweeping dust from the road. His hand never drifted far from his sword.

"That went clean," he said quietly.

"Did you expect it not to?" I asked.

"Clean doesn't always mean simple," he replied. "He'll tell himself he did it for his sons."

"He did," I said. "But he made a deal with the Devil. That doesn't make it better."

Sariel huffed an almost-laugh. "No."

Lilith loosened her hold on my arm but stayed close, matching my stride without looking like she was trying to. Vespera moved on her other side, shoulders brushing occasionally, gravity disguised as coincidence.

From the fire temple on the hill, I could feel attention scraping over us, like the prickle of a stare between my shoulder blades. Priests watching from their steps. Acolytes pretending not to see.

"They're deciding what to call this," Lilith murmured, eyes on the distant altar. "You here. Him there. All of this." She made a small circle in the air with her free hand.

"They already picked a name," I said. "Angra Mainyu, the adversary." I smiled, letting it go knife-sharp for anyone watching from afar. "They're not subtle."

I was simply the shadow they needed to make His Light look brighter.

Lilith hummed, amused. "Names can be rewritten," she said.

"Planning a rebrand?" I asked.

"Always," she said. "I like having options."

Vespera's mouth curled, like that answer pleased her.

We walked in silence for a stretch, the sun beating down, the city's noise a low, constant thrum. A boy carrying water paused at a doorway as we passed, curiosity pushing him a step too close. His gaze snagged on Vespera's horns, then dropped to Lilith's bared teeth, then to my sword. He didn't bow. He just stared.

Lilith's lips parted, amused. "You should

kneel," she told him gently. "It's better for the knees than being forced down."

The boy flinched and dropped so fast his jug sloshed.

I didn't say anything, but I watched the way she watched him, calculating, but not cruel. She liked to take measure, filing away what fear looked like in this place, how far it could bend before it broke. She was learning this world, not for me, but for herself.

By the time we reached the hidden break between realms, the priests had gone back to pretending we didn't exist. The city exhaled, just a little, like a man who realized the knife at his throat had moved away but wasn't quite sheathed yet.

I tore the air open. Hell's heat rolled through at once, thick and cloying after the dry burn of the Persian sun. Stone replaced stone. Smoke changed flavor. The faint scent of incense gave way to sulfur and iron, and the simmering breath of the rivers.

Lilith released my arm as we crossed back over. Vespera fell into easy conversation with her immediately, their heads bent close, laughter low and private. Vespera reached up and adjusted a fold of Lilith's veil with unthinking intimacy, fingers lingering a second longer than necessary. Neither of them looked at me.

Sariel did. Just once. Just enough. "You want me to keep an eye on him?" he asked quietly, meaning the merchant, the deal, the inevitable fallout.

"Yes," I said. Then, after a beat, quieter, "And her."

His gaze flicked toward Lilith and Vespera, then back. He didn't ask which *her* I meant. He was clever enough to know it was both.

"How close?" he asked.

"Close enough they don't notice," I said. "Far enough, you don't get caught."

He nodded once. "Understood."

I started walking toward the central halls. Lilith glanced back over her shoulder, caught my eye, and smiled like the morning had gone exactly the way she'd wanted.

"Successful outing," she called. "We should go more often. It suits you."

I gave her the ghost of a smile in return, just enough to keep the game even. "Maybe," I said. "We'll see."

She laughed, pleased, and let Vespera pull her down a different corridor.

I watched them go until they turned the corner. Two shadows moving together. My castle, my realm, my supposed queen, and her new favorite.

Everyone else saw stability. A united front. The adversary, flanked by his chosen. But I had stopped seeing it as *us* at all when I started wondering what, exactly, Lilith was building that didn't require me in it.

CHAPTER SEVEN

Lucifer

By the time Sariel found me, the screaming had already changed.

Hell had a thousand kinds of screaming. Rage. Terror. Begging. That thin, high sound people made when they realized the pain wasn't going to stop just because they couldn't think through it anymore.

This wasn't that. This was layered, overlapping, every voice trying to crawl over the next one.

"They're getting out," Sariel said.

I looked up from the map of Hell I'd been carving into the stone arm of the throne. "Who?"

"Acheron." His jaw was tight, eyes a little brighter than usual. "The river's losing souls. The banks are… wrong."

Sariel didn't rattle easily. If he looked like

that, something was breaking that shouldn't.

I pushed to my feet. "Show me."

We didn't walk. Sariel flexed his fingers in that precise little pattern he'd taught no one else, and the corridor obeyed. The hall stretched, then folded, doors and arches sliding past in a blur as distance kinked in on itself. Spaces shortened because he told them to. Hell liked to impress me, but it moved for Sariel.

The first hint of Acheron was the mist.

It crept into the corridor ahead of us, thin and silver, curling around our ankles, whispering against the stone like someone trying to hush a crowd. The closer we got, the louder the sound grew, a roar with teeth hidden in it.

Then the hall spat us out onto the overlooking ledge, and the river filled everything. It writhed below, black and wide and overfull. Souls thrashed in the water, pale limbs flashing in the dark, clawing over each other, dragging one another down, and still trying to climb. They were supposed to sink. To be claimed. Acheron existed to hold what couldn't be trusted to lie still.

Instead, they were making it halfway up the banks.

We watched as three of them hauled themselves out at once. Hands scraped against slick rock, nails peeling back. One slipped, taking the two others with him. But another found a crack, fingers wedging deep, tendons standing out in his forearms as he dragged his chest onto the stone.

There were guards, of course. Demons stationed along the banks with hooks and barbed poles, legs braced, tails lashing. But they were losing ground. For every soul they knocked back, three more took its place.

"Why?" I asked quietly.

"The river's too full," Sariel said. "We've been diverting more souls here than Styx can take. The original flows weren't designed for this."

Of course they weren't. The First Light had built His afterlife for neat stories and simple morality. Heaven was for a chosen handful who looked good in hymns and tidy parables. Everyone else slid here by default, good or bad. He'd never planned for what happened when almost no one earned the Light He promised. Instead, all of them piled up in the dark.

I stepped off the ledge. Sariel didn't try to stop me. Gravity was merely a suggestion here anyway. The drop was short, the air humid with fog as I fell until the stone rose to meet me.

My boots hit the bank, and the nearest

souls flinched—some in horror, some in hope. I felt both like a draft.

One of the demons turned, panting, black blood slicking his forearms. "My liege," he gasped. "They're—"

"I can see what they're doing," I said.

He snapped his mouth shut as he quickly bowed his head and went back to work, shoving his hook into the shoulder of a man who'd gotten his whole torso onto the shore and yanking him back into the water.

It didn't help. Not enough. The river wasn't a punishment anymore. It was a fucking riot.

I walked to the edge and stepped in. Acheron climbed my boots, my calves, wrapping itself around my legs. It wasn't cold. It was worse, dense and clinging, a weight that sank deeper than bone. Mist coiled around my waist, trying to climb higher, trying to find a way in.

Hands grabbed at me immediately. They didn't care who I was. Anything above the waterline was a ladder. Fingers dug into my thighs, my hips, my belt. Someone's hand slid along my ribs toward my shoulder, nails scraping, desperate.

They all felt the same. Wet. Slippery. Pleading.

"Enough," I said.

The word dropped like a stone. For a

heartbeat, the river stilled. The roar thinned to a low boil under the surface. The grasping hands loosened, not in obedience, just in confusion.

I looked down. Most of them still scrabbled and lunged, still tearing into each other for another inch of rock, another breath of air they weren't owed. But not all of them.

There were some who hung just below the surface, barely moving. They weren't fighting or helping. They were just… watching. Their eyes were open wide under the black water, tracking everything — the clumps of souls, the guards, me.

They were bystanders. The ones who'd always let everyone else drown first and do absolutely nothing. Of course, it would be them.

I reached into the water and closed my hand around the wrist of one of them. The soul I dragged up came apart, skin sloughing off in my grip, and reassembled as his head broke the surface, struggling to remember what shape it should take. Water poured from his mouth in a ragged cough. He clawed for the bank, same as the others.

"Not up," I said quietly, tightening my grip as he scrabbled at my arm. "Sideways."

He didn't understand. That was fine. This wasn't for him anyway.

I hauled him onto the rock until he lay half out of the river, still dripping, chest heaving. One of the demons took an uncertain step toward us, hook half-raised.

I flicked my fingers. He froze where he stood as I planted my foot against the soul's sternum and pressed him flat.

His eyes found mine, wild, furious. "Please," he gasped. "I—I can work, I can—"

"You already did nothing," I said. "That's why I picked you."

He tried to twist away. I sank my other hand back into Acheron. The river rose to meet it. Black water climbed my wrist, threading between my fingers, thick as oil and eager to stain. It surged up my arm with a kind of greedy relief, like it had been waiting for someone to tell it what to do. When I pushed my hand down against the soul's chest, Acheron went with it.

He screamed. Pain, terror, both. It didn't matter. His body bowed off the stone and then collapsed. The water didn't pour out of him. It poured into him, deeper than lungs, deeper than bone, straight into whatever stubborn knot passed for self.

His edges blurred as flesh leeched to shadow. Bone elongated, joints popping and reforming where no human anatomy had ever intended them. Arms stretched and thinned, fingers unspooling into something long and hooked, more branch than hand. Color bled out of him until he was swallowed in shades of black, darker even than the river.

A hood drew itself over his head, not cloth but condensed night, pulling down over the place where a face should've been. For a beat, features tried to form beneath it—eyes, a mouth, a nose—twisting, melting, finally collapsing inward to leave only a hollow. A pit of layered absence.

His form rose, and his feet sank into the bank. Like roots.

Thin threads of Acheron ran from his ankles back into the riverbed, tethering him to the current. I felt it, taut and permanent, like the river had grabbed him back and decided to wear him instead of losing him.

This new… thing lifted its head. The hollow where its eyes weren't turned toward the water. The mist thickened around it, clinging like devotion.

"Look at them," I said softly. "Really look."
It did.
The low sound that started in its chest wasn't a scream. It wasn't a voice. It was pressure, a hum that vibrated through the stone into my boots, up through my spine, buzzing behind my teeth. The river answered, churning, then settling into a new rhythm

that matched it.

A soul lunged for the shore to our right, fingers digging into a crack. Without a word from me, the new thing on the bank moved.

It didn't step. It glided, a tall, cloaked shape hovering just above the stone, water streaming from its shrouded form in thin, evaporating ribbons. One long arm unwrapped from the folds of its darkness, ending in a hooked suggestion of a hand.

It caught the escaping soul by the spine. The scream that tore out of the drowning thing's throat was heartbreakingly human.

The Watcher—because that's what it was, even before I named it—pushed him back down into the water with terrible gentleness. No flourish. No lingering. Just inevitability.

"That's one," I said.

I did it again. And again.

Each time, I chose the ones who'd watched their own lives burn and done nothing. The ones who'd stood at the edges of other people's disasters and decided stillness was safety. I dragged them out, pressed my hand to their chests, plunged the other back into the river, and let Acheron choose with me.

Drown. Or watch.

Every soul the river chose to watch came out wrong in the same way.

Tall. Shrouded. Cloaked in shifting strands

of shadow and bone, edges always moving, never quite settling. Faces erased beneath their hoods, no eyes, no mouths, just those deep, hollow pits that drank in everything and gave nothing back. Their feet anchored to the banks, tendrils of dark water running from their ankles into the riverbed like veins.

The hum grew with each one, a layered vibration that set the mist trembling and made the guards flinch.

By the time I stepped back out of the water, clothes heavy and dripping, the banks were lined with them.

They stood in a loose, uneven row, some half in the river, some half on the shore, all of them oriented toward the current. Broken shadows above the rocks, gliding a few inches off the ground when they moved, cloaks dragging through the black surface.

Even I refused to look directly into the hollows where their faces weren't. You never should, not even me.

"Your penalty's this," I told them, my voice carrying easily over the newly-muted roar of Acheron. "You watched in life and did nothing. You'll watch properly now. Every soul that reaches. Every hand that slips. You'll feel it all, and you won't get to look away."

The hum deepened, a low, almost-subsonic agreement.

Stone scraped above. I didn't have to turn to know who it was.

"How efficient," Lilith said.

I glanced back.

She stood on the higher ledge, bare-shouldered in her usual silk gown that poured over her body, dragging a dark little train that streaked the stone like fresh blood in the thin river light. Vespera hovered just behind her, expression caught between awe and something more clinical.

"Where've you been?" I asked.

She just smiled. "You didn't invite me."

True. I hadn't.

She descended the steps barefoot with unhurried grace, careful not to disturb the mist, though it lapped at her ankles like it wanted a taste. Vespera followed, boots silent, gaze flicking over the Watchers as if she were cataloging each one.

Lilith stopped just short of the waterline. Her eyes moved from me, soaked and half-submerged, to the nearest Watcher. It loomed at the edge of her reach, tall and still, cloak dripping, head tilted toward the river as if listening for the next escape attempt.

"You pulled souls out of the river," she said quietly. "And then made them part of it."

"I made them useful," I said. "Acheron couldn't hold them all. Now it doesn't have to."

Her mouth curved, impressed despite herself. "You solved three problems at once," she said. "Containment. Punishment. And you've given the river eyes."

Vespera's attention sharpened at that. "Not just eyes," she murmured. "They're anchored. They feel every soul that touches the banks. That's… a lot of information."

I shot her a look.

She lifted her shoulders in a small shrug. "I'm simply observing."

Lilith's gaze lingered on the thin threads of dark water tethering the Watchers to the current. "Do they report to you?" she asked. "Directly?"

"Everything here reports to me," I said.

"That's not what I asked."

I met her eyes. "They're bound to the river first," I said. "Then to me. That's enough."

She held my gaze a heartbeat longer than necessary. "For now," she said softly.

Down in the water, a knot of souls surged toward the shore, sensing distraction. Three of the new Watchers slid forward in eerie unison, cloaks billowing without wind. They herded the souls back with a few efficient movements, long arms extending, hooked hands guiding rather than striking.

No words were needed. There was no

hesitation. It was… functional.

"You're good at this," Lilith said, studying my profile instead of the river now.

"At what?" I asked.

"Taking what's broken and rearranging it so it can't break in the same way again," she said. "Even if you have to make something terrible to do it."

"That is Hell," I said. "It contained before me. And it will endure because of me."

She huffed a soft laugh. "You sound like a king when you say things like that."

"I am a king," I said. "Last I checked."

Her smile didn't quite reach her eyes. "Some kings only wear the crown," she said. "You're building the walls that keep it from falling off."

Vespera glanced between us, noting every word.

The Watchers hummed, the river rolled, and the guards slowly remembered their hooks and their orders.

Up on the ledge, Sariel appeared again, eyes going straight to the changed banks. For a moment, something like pride flickered across his face before he smoothed it away.

"You fixed it," he said.

"For now," I answered, echoing Lilith's earlier tone.

He looked at the Watchers, at the way they stood motionless until something moved, then glided into place like they'd been doing this for centuries. "What are they?" he asked.

"Watchers," I said. "The ones who used to stand still while everyone else drowned. I've given them a vantage point they can't walk away from anymore."

He nodded slowly. "They'll keep the river in line."

"That's the idea."

Lilith's eyes were still on the tethering threads, fingers twitching like she wanted to touch one and see what it did. "And if something... interfered with those?" she asked lightly. "If someone wanted to... redirect what they see?"

I stepped out of the water and onto the bank in front of her, close enough that the damp from my clothes darkened the hem of her dress.

"Then they'd discover," I said, my voice dropping until even the water seemed to listen, "that Acheron and I are in perfect agreement."

A pulse rippled through the current.

"We don't forgive meddling."

Her smile sharpened. "There it is," she murmured. "The part they don't write into the stories."

She brushed her hand through my hair, smoothing it back from my face as if I were something half-wild that had allowed her close. The gesture looked intimate.

It felt like ownership. And yet for a moment, I almost leaned into it.

"Which part?"

"The line between what you'll tolerate and what you'll burn," she said.

"I thought that was obvious."

"Not to them," she said, tipping her head toward the other realms. "To them, you're the chaos. The sabotage. The thing that ruins order."

"Maybe I am," I said.

Lilith's gaze flicked back to the Watchers. "No," she said quietly. "You're the enforcement. You're the order. They just don't realize it yet."

Vespera watched me like I was another system to diagram.

The river rolled on, contained. The Watchers stood their vigil, tall and shrouded, humming softly as every soul that brushed the banks sent a fresh shiver of sensation through them.

Sariel began issuing quiet orders to the guards, and for the first time since I'd taken the throne, Acheron didn't look like something I was barely keeping up with. It looked like something I'd designed on purpose.

It should've felt like victory. Instead, something cold slid into place in my chest as Lilith and Vespera turned away together, heads bent close, their voices slipping back to me on the river mist.

"If they feel everything that touches the banks," Vespera murmured, "…can use that. It's a net… not just a prison."

"Exactly," Lilith said, pleased. "…those eyes and not one of them asking… really watching for."

The satisfaction I'd expected never came as they disappeared up the steps, swallowed by shadow. I hadn't just built a new layer of Hell. I'd given it sight. But Lilith was already thinking in terms of access.

I could've called her back. Pressed her. Forced the conversation into the open. But proof doesn't survive confrontation. That's when it goes to hide. So I let her go. If she had always been playing a longer game, which I was beginning to suspect, I wanted to see the board.

CHAPTER EIGHT

Lucifer

I woke to the wrong kind of cold.

Hell had its own temperatures. The radiant heat of the lower forges. The damp chill that clung to the deeper caverns. The oppressive, humid breath of the rivers. This wasn't any of those.

This was bone-cold and still, threaded under the air like a vein of ice.

I opened my eyes. A Watcher stood in the corner of my bedchamber.

It hovered inches above the floor, shrouded in that not-quite-cloth, its long, boneless limbs wrapped in shadow and suggestion of bone. No face, just the familiar hollow where features refused to form, sucking in the dim firelight without reflecting any of it back. The hem of its cloak trailed a thin smear of moisture along the stone, as if it had just stepped out of the river and hadn't noticed.

It shouldn't have been here. The Acheron was miles of twisting path away, time and distance both bent around it so nothing could ever stumble there by accident. They were tethered to the river, and I'd never pulled a Watcher from its post. Never given them leave to move without the river under their feet.

The low hum echoed behind my teeth and throbbed like a headache.

I pushed myself up on one elbow, sheets pooling at my waist. "You're a long way from home," I said.

The Watcher didn't flinch or even bow. They never did. Their obedience wasn't performance. It was a function. Its hooded head tilted, hollow pits settling on me.

"Back," I told it.

There was always that moment when you gave a new order to a new creation, the fractional pause while power checked the chain of command. Usually, it was instant, Acheron answering with eager compliance.

This time, there was a hitch. It wasn't long or even obvious, just a single, unnatural beat of hesitation, like something else had its hands on the same rope and wasn't sure whether to let go.

The hum scraped higher. Then the Watcher vanished. No swirl of cloak, no dramatic exit.

One moment it existed, and the next, it was simply part of elsewhere, the air in the corner warming by a degree, as if it had taken the cold with it.

I swung my legs over the side of the bed, my feet finding stone. The echo of the tether still burned in my palm, a phantom sensation from where I'd gripped the first Watcher in the Acheron. I closed my eyes and followed it backward.

Down, first. Through the castle foundations, through layers of basalt and buried screams, into the thick, slow pulse of the river. I felt the familiar weight of the river, dark and heavy, wrapping around everything that was mine there. The tethers from each Watcher arching into it, hundreds of thin, taut lines anchoring them to the current and the bank.

Then sideways, along the one that had just warmed my chamber. I found it there. The point where it had bent enough to let the Watcher slip. A knot of resistance that wasn't mine. The river's claim came in hot and sure. My own grip sat over it, dominant, absolute.

But over both was a third thread that wasn't mine. It was thin and high. Reaching up, but not to any part of Hell. It went up past the crust of the realm, past the twisted boundaries where souls and realities tangle, past the firmament. And toward something bright and cold and smug with its own divinity.

That sensation made my stomach twist.

Of course. Of fucking course, they couldn't leave it alone. I'd given Hell eyes, and someone had decided they should point upward.

I didn't rip it out. Not yet. I pinched it between my metaphorical fingers and felt along its length. There was residue there, the psychic equivalent of fingerprints. Not just Lilith's or Vespera's. It was also… older. Familiar. Unmistakably… Him.

I cut the thread cleanly at the Watcher's end, right where it tried to splice into my system, and let the rest snap back toward whatever angel that had been listening. The sudden silence along that line was satisfying in a way that made me want to smile. The hum in my teeth dropped to its usual low, steady buzz.

Someone knocked on the outer door.

The timing would have been suspicious if it weren't Sariel. He knocked like that even when we were in the middle of an apocalypse. He'd probably knock like that if Heaven fell into this place in flames.

"Come in," I said.

The door opened without a sound. Sariel slipped inside, closing it behind him. He'd dressed already—dark leathers, sword strapped to his back, hair pulled away from his face. Only his eyes betrayed how fast he'd been moving.

"You felt it," he said.

"Which part?" I asked.

"Acheron." He hesitated, then added, "And… something else."

I studied him. "What did you see?"

He moved closer, but not too close. Sariel understood the radius of my temper better than most.

"The banks have been… glitching," he said. "Only for a breath at a time. The Watchers flicker. One moment they're there, the next they're… half-there. Like something's trying to pull them in two directions."

"How long?"

"Since yesterday," he said. "Maybe longer. We only started noticing when the guards reported gaps in coverage. They'd blink, and a Watcher would be a few feet away from where it had been."

"And you thought it was just the system settling," I said.

His jaw flexed. "I thought it might be growing pains," he admitted. "New structures do that. But this morning, one of them disappeared entirely for the space of a breath. It reappeared up here."

He flicked his gaze to the corner where the Watcher had stood.

"You saw it?" I asked.

"Felt it," he said. "Paths stretched when they shouldn't have. I was on my way when it… resolved."

He didn't ask what it had been doing in my chambers—professionalism, or tact, or both.

"There is someone else attempting to control them," I said. "Or there was. Not anymore."

Sariel went very still. "From above?" he asked.

"Possibly."

His mouth flattened. "I suspected, but I wanted actual evidence I could bring you. But if you're sure, I can lock the paths from this side," he said. "Force all movement to route only through you."

"There's no need," I said. "I've already cut their access to this one."

He exhaled slowly. "All right. But the pattern still worries me. Someone's testing boundaries."

Someone always was.

"Keep watching," I said. "Note every flicker. Every absence."

He nodded. "Do you want me at the river?"

"Not yet."

Sariel inclined his head and withdrew, leaving me alone with the fading chill and the memory of a Watcher where it shouldn't have been.

I stared at the ceiling, thinking about all the times I'd spent telling myself Lilith and I were just two sides of the same coin. Both rejected. Both were thrown out of the story when we stopped fitting the parts He'd written for us. This whole time, it had made what we were easier to carry if I believed that.

But the last few centuries had started to sour that story.

It wasn't the questions she asked me. It was the way I heard my answers come out of her mouth later, trimmed and sharpened, handed to Vespera like pieces of a puzzle they were putting together without me. Little comments about what I could do, what I wouldn't do, where I hesitated, dressed up as casual observations, and then that riverside conversation I'd overheard between them. All talk of "nets" and "information" and how the Watchers might be "useful" to someone listening.

If I lined it all up, it stopped feeling like wounded solidarity and started looking a lot more like an assignment.

Watch him. See if he remembers. Fine. Two could play at that.

I took the long way to Acheron. Without Sariel, there was no path-warping this time. No shortcuts. Just corridors and stairs and the slow descent through the realm.

I didn't care if everyone thought I was brooding. Let rumors chase each other through the halls if they want. Hell loved a story. And I could use that.

By the time I reached the last bend before the river's overlook, the air was thick with mist. It clung to the stone like cobwebs, tasting faintly of iron and old fear.

Voices drifted ahead. Not the roar of souls or the low hum of the Watchers. It was softer and measured.

I stepped into the shadow of a column and let the stone lean around me, just enough to blur my presence. Not invisibility. Just misdirection. If someone looked, they'd see what they expected to see. And nobody expected to find the King of the Damned pressed against the wall like a man listening at a door.

Down on the bank, Vespera stood alone, if you didn't count the eight-foot-tall horror looming a pace away from her, half in the water, half on the stone. The Watcher towered over her. Its cloaked form was as still as carved night. Mist curled around its ankles, drawn to the thin tether of dark water running from its feet into the riverbed. It should've been ignoring her. It should've been ignoring everything but the souls trying to escape the river.

She stood almost close enough to touch it. Her horns caught what little light there was, against the fog. She wore simple leathers, practical, the kind that wouldn't snag if you had to run or fight. Her hands were bare.

"You feel them, don't you?" she murmured.

Her voice carried strangely, riding the mist.

"You feel every one of them who brushes the bank. Every single one that tries to claw its way out. All that noise, all that wanting."

The Watcher didn't move. It didn't need to. The tether at its ankles quivered, a tiny, tremoring line.

Vespera smiled, small and sharp. "It's a lot," she said. "Too much for one mind, even if it's already dead. You shouldn't have to hold it alone."

She lifted her hand, stopping just short of the tether. Fingers hung there, hovering over the liquid shadow, careful not to make contact.

"And you don't," she whispered. "Not really. Do you?"

The hum spiked. It felt like standing too close to a struck bell.

For a heartbeat, I saw it, not with my eyes

but with whatever sense I'd wired into the river when I created them. A pulse. A ping. A little flare of attention racing up the tether, away from the water, away from me. Reaching.

Vespera lowered her hand, satisfied. "Good," she said. "You're listening."

She turned and walked back up the bank, boots soundless on the damp stone. The Watcher went still again as its tether trembled once, then steadied.

I stayed where I was until I was sure she was gone. Then I went down to the water. The other Watchers registered me immediately. The hum along the banks dropped into a lower register, threads tightening, all those hollow, absent faces orienting toward me without turning.

I picked the one she'd been talking to. Its tether tasted faintly of her, like ozone clinging to metal after lightning.

"Someone's been teaching you bad habits," I said.

It didn't answer. It couldn't. That wasn't how I'd made them. But the tether trembled a fraction. I knelt and pressed my hand to the black thread of water, tying it to Acheron. Power flowed up at once, eager to fill the point of contact.

"New rule," I said.

The river stirred.

"You still watch," I told it. "You still feel. You still drag every reaching hand back where it belongs. But if anything tries to pull what you see past me, past the river, past Hell —you route it somewhere else first."

It shuddered, uncertain.

"To me," I said. "You give it to me before you give it to anyone else."

The current surged, dark and pleased. The tether at the Watcher's ankles brightened in my inner sight, the thin upward line that had snapped away earlier wrapping around the thicker, darker cable that bound it to the river and to me.

"I won't stop them talking," I murmured. "I'll just make sure I hear every word."

The hum settled into a new chord as I straightened and stepped back. The Watcher resumed its position, sensing the next escape attempt, as if nothing had changed. But I'd braided myself into the extra thread now. Whatever message they'd tried to send would hit me first.

Lilith could think her little minion wired a backchannel. A backchannel I was sure was going to The First Light. Let Him think His eye had found a way in. I'd spent ages being the story they told. It was time I started editing their script.

That same night, the first report came in, and Lilith had never come to bed. She was probably with Vespera again. But I wasn't asleep. I hadn't bothered trying. And sleep in Hell was less about rest and more about refusing to listen to everything that wanted your attention. Tonight, there were too many things I wasn't ready to ignore.

I sat in the dark with my back to the cold stone wall of my private inner chamber, one knee drawn up, palm resting loosely against it. No candles. No conjured light. Just the soft glow of faraway fire through the high, narrow window in the wall and the distant murmur of the realm breathing.

The hum started in my teeth, climbed behind my eyes, then slid sideways. For a moment, I was back on Acheron's banks, feeling every drag and slip of the drowning souls through the Watchers' senses.

Then the perspective tilted, sharp and dizzying. I was looking up. Not with my own eyes. With theirs. Through one of them, standing rooted where I'd left it. The river at its feet with the dark stretching overhead.

A thread uncoiled from the tether and reached, not physically, but in the way prayers reached, in the way fear did when it realized it was out of options. It slid through the cracks between realms, up through the layers of creation like smoke through stone.

I followed as the air thinned, the heat turning cool. The static of worship clogged everything, a thousand whispered invocations clinging to a single name—His—the First Light.

The thread brushed against something vast and bright and utterly uninterested in the individual parts of its own machine. A great presence pressed back along it. It wasn't quite attention, just awareness.

And then there was a voice, but it wasn't His. It was… hers.

"Father," Lilith said, her tone smooth, practiced. "He doesn't remember."

Her words slid along the thread, carried without sound. I heard them anyway.

"He's building systems," she went on. "Rivers. Boundaries. Creatures that enforce the rules. He's creating Hell. He thinks it's defiance, but it looks a lot like obedience, doesn't it?"

Pressure warmed along the line. Approval. Or something like it.

"He's powerful," she continued. "More than they know down there. His reach is growing. But there's no… crack yet. No sign. No recognition when he looks at the places that should hurt."

"Good," He answered. But it wasn't words.

It was structured intent. "He must not remember. But if he does, you will tell me that very moment."

I tasted arrogance in it. And beneath it was her tightly contained vigilance.

Lilith replied at once. "Always. I'll keep watching."

The transmission began to withdraw, but I couldn't let it leave clean. I signaled the Watcher to hold the seam open—just a fraction of a second longer than it should have remained stable.

The channel wasn't mystical. It was directional—a focused line of awareness connecting her mind to His. I locked onto it, not by reaching, but by aligning. I narrowed my own awareness to match its frequency, just like the pattern of thought it carried. Once aligned, the channel registered me as ambient interference rather than intrusion.

Then I traced it backward. Every transmission leaves a trace. It wasn't sound or an image, but an impression, a faint psychic signature. That was what He read, so I removed it.

By the time it reached wherever He was listening from, it was thinner, duller. It was stripped of some of its detail, and enough remained to keep her in His good graces. Not enough to give Him the full measure of what I was building.

There was no trace, no distortion. There was no evidence that I had been listening. Then I let the Watcher release the seam. The channel sealed, and somewhere far above this realm, He remained convinced His surveillance was intact. And I was back in my chamber, hand clenched around my own knee hard enough to make my skin bleed.

Father. Lilith had never told me she spoke to Him that way. Of course, she hadn't. She wanted Him to choose her, and the easiest way was to play into me always being the adversary in His story, the shadow that made His light look brighter. Ambition. Pride.

A clean sin they could point at and say, "That's why."

Why did He care so much? If the official story were enough, He wouldn't need to put someone in my bed to report on what I did or didn't remember.

So there was something else. Something under that lie. Something He was still afraid might surface. Afraid enough to send His most wounded daughter into my realm and tell her to watch me for cracks.

I sat there in the dark for a long time, listening to Hell breathe around me, feeling the faint hum of the Watchers at the edge of my perception. Then I stood.

She was waiting in our rooms, sprawled across the bed like she owned it. Her favorite red silk clung to her curves, the slip dress cut low enough that it was only pretending to cover her breasts and high enough to make modesty a distant rumor.

She'd arranged herself deliberately, I could tell. One leg bent, a long line of bare skin clean up to her hip visible through the parted fabric, her hair a dark spill around her shoulders.

"There you are," she said, like I'd merely stepped out for a drink and not spent hours wiring a river into obedience. "I was starting to think you'd married that Garden and forgotten to tell me."

"Not quite," I said.

She chuckled, low. "Mm. Well, I've also been… occupied." Her smile flashed, all fang and implication. "Whatever you were doing, the screaming changed. I assume that was you, not a coincidence."

She patted the bed between her knees. "Come here."

I walked to the edge of the mattress. She sat up, closing the distance, fingers brushing my wrist, my forearm, my chest. Her touch was cool, always, the kind of cold that invited heat out of spite.

"You're tense," she observed. "Did our little

creations misbehave?"

"My creations," I corrected. "You just flirted with one."

She laughed. "Vespera's curious," she said. "She likes your toys. I like watching her play with them."

Her hands slid up to my shoulders. If I looked down, I'd see fangs, not lips. I didn't look down.

"What do they feel?" she murmured. "The Watchers. When they stand there and hold all that drowning. Does it bleed into you when you call them?"

"Why?" I asked.

She let the question roll off her. "Because you're entangled," she said. "You and the river. You and the Garden. You and this whole infernal clockwork. I want to know where it stops, and you begin."

Her eyes were very dark when she said it.

"You could've just asked," I said.

"I am asking," she replied. Her thumbs traced circles just above my collarbones, deceptively tender. "Do they follow if you call them into other places? Can they see for you anywhere, or only on the banks?"

They follow wherever I tell them, I almost said.

Instead, I said, "I made river guards, not hounds. I don't need eyes everywhere."

A lie, neatly folded around a sliver of truth. The best kind.

"Mm." She made a considering sound. "Shame. It'd be useful."

"I already know everything I need to," I said.

"I wouldn't be so sure," she murmured.

I caught her wrists, hard but not enough to bruise, just enough to stop those cool fingers from tracing any more lines over my skin.

"You've been talking to Him," I said.

Her pupils widened, as if the room had darkened. "Who?" she asked.

"Don't insult both of us," I said. "You asked if I remembered. You asked if I was trying to rebuild something from above. Now you've got your hands in my river, and my Watchers are blinking in and out of my chambers. You don't have to say His name. I can feel it."

Silence stretched between us. Then she smiled, slowly. It was wary and almost admiring. "You weren't supposed to notice that," she said softly.

"I notice everything in my realm," I replied. "Eventually."

Her gaze searched my face the moment I stepped into the room. "You don't remember," she said softly. "Do you?"

It wasn't a question, and something in me snapped.

In the space between one breath and the next, I crossed the room, the floor shuddering faintly beneath my steps. The bedposts rattled as my hand struck the mattress beside her shoulder.

My wings flared wide behind me without my permission, dark and massive, filling the chamber with the low rush of displaced air.

"Remember what, Lilith?" I demanded, punctuating each word.

I loomed over her, my shadow swallowing the torchlights. The heat rolling off me made the silk sheets shift against her skin.

For a moment, she didn't move. Then she lifted her chin slightly, meeting my gaze without flinching. Defiant. The corner of her mouth curved.

"Well," she said lazily, her voice turning warm and dangerous, "this is much more interesting than anything else you've done lately."

Her fingers slid slowly up my arm, where it braced beside her. Something hungry flickered over her features, gone before it could settle.

"Hmm," she breathed, more to herself than to me. "If I'd known anger made you this attentive," she murmured, "I might've provoked you sooner."

The tension in the room twisted, no longer a

blade aimed at her throat. Now it was something else entirely. Then she leaned up and kissed me.

It was all sharp softness, lips and teeth, and the faint hint of copper that always lived on her tongue. Her body pressed against mine, cold where I was warm, silk whispering between us. Her hands slid free of my grip and up into my hair, pulling, anchoring.

I let her. I let her pull me over her onto the bed, let her dress pool around us, let her distract and seduce and soothe. I touched her where she wanted to be touched, held her the way she liked to be held, and said the filthy things she loved to hear.

We went through the motions we'd taught each other, the choreography of power wrapped in pleasure.

On the surface, nothing changed. Underneath, everything did. Because now, when she curled against me afterward, her head on my chest, her fingers drawing idle patterns along my ribs, and when she asked, casually, "Do you ever feel anything… missing, when you look at what you've built?" I didn't answer honestly.

"No," I said, staring at the ceiling. "Hell is exactly what it needs to be."

The bond between us warmed, pleased by our alignment. She hummed, content, and closed her eyes.

I lay there, wide awake, listening to her breathe, feeling the faint, distant hum of the Watchers at the edge of my senses. Somewhere, one of them would blink, its tether tugged by her hand or His. Whatever they sent, whatever words she dressed her reports in, would hit me first now. Let her keep talking. Let Him keep listening.

The real mistake hadn't been trusting her with information. It had been letting her in deep enough to bind our power and our blood together, like that made us untouchable instead of making me easier to infiltrate.

This was the stupidest thing I've ever done, I thought, feeling the shared power coil tight between us. But just as I felt myself start to slip under, I vowed to myself that one day soon, I was going to break it. Every thread. Every drop of her in me and mine in her.

They wanted me to be the adversary. Fine. I'd start by undoing the bond they'd hidden their spy inside and make sure she was the one who bled for it.

CHAPTER NINE

Lucifer

I wore a groove in the floor before I realized I'd started pacing.

My private chamber wasn't large, not compared to the throne room or the strategy halls, but tonight it felt too big and too small at once. Too much space to walk, not enough space to think. Stone walls, low fire, a single narrow window opening onto the darkness. A bed I hadn't bothered to lie in.

The bond pulsed, a low, steady thrum under my skin. A reminder of who I was tied to.

Lilith was asleep somewhere in the castle, or pretending to be. Either way, I felt her, the way you feel an old wound when the weather changes. Power threaded between us, blood answering blood. Every time I pulled away from it, it tugged back, a quiet, possessive insistence, a web of shared channels running through my power, hers braided into mine and mine braided into hers. Our bite marks had faded, but the bond hadn't. It would outlast teeth and skin and maybe us if I didn't do something about it.

The problem was simple to say and nearly impossible to solve. How do you break a blood bond with someone who lies in your bed, rules at your side, and reports your every crack to the god who cast you out… without letting her feel the knife coming?

I ran a hand through my hair and turned again.

Options marched through my head and fell apart just as quickly. I could rip it all at once, brute-force, tear the connection down to the root. The backlash would be catastrophic. She'd feel it before I finished the first tear. She'd know I knew something, and she'd go straight to Him.

I could starve it, but would that break it? Stop feeding power through it, let it wither. But bonds like this didn't just carry power. They carried information. Intent. Emotion. If I suddenly went blank, she'd notice. She was many things, but stupid wasn't one of them.

I could pretend nothing was wrong and do nothing at all. That might have been the worst option.

I stopped in the middle of the chamber and pressed my thumb hard against the center of my palm where we'd first sliced ourselves, as if I could bruise the memory out.

I'd broken oaths before. Broken covenants, pacts, and even the occasional city. But I'd never broken a bond like this. Not one that tangled so deeply through my own power, I couldn't tell where it ended, and I began.

A knock broke my spiraling. Three measured taps that were neither hurried nor hesitant. Just… precise.

Sariel.

"Come in," I said.

The door opened on a breath of cooler air from the corridor. Sariel slipped inside, closing it softly behind him. He was already armed, a sword across his back, clothes dark and practical, hair pulled back from his face. The only sign he'd been moving fast was the faint flush high on his cheeks.

"Sorry," he said. "I know you prefer not to be disturbed when you're…" His gaze flicked briefly to the worn path on the floor between the wall and the window. "…doing whatever that is."

"Thinking," I said.

He arched a brow. "Violently," he said. "You pacing a hole in the floor usually means something's gone wrong."

"Has it?" I asked. "Or did you come here to tell me everything's perfectly fine and I can go back to being a very decorative statue?"

"Not exactly," he said.

So, wrong, then.

I exhaled through my teeth. "What now?"

Stepping further into the room, he said, "The river's… changing. And not in a way anyone asked for."

My jaw tightened. "Which river?"

"You know which," he said quietly.

I did. That was the problem.

Lethe moved differently from the others. Acheron dragged grief. Styx bound oaths. The others tore, burned, and reflected. Lethe was different. Lethe forgot. It ate edges first. Then details. Then whole thoughts, until there was nothing left but a body that used to remember how to be someone.

I'd built it, and I still refused to step into it. Watching people drown in their own oblivion was one thing. Feeling it strip my own memories away was another.

"Explain," I said.

"The souls on the banks are… wrong," Sariel said. "They're losing things they shouldn't. Not just life memories. Structural things. Language. Basic fear. Some are going… blank."

"Blank how?"

He searched for the word. "They're not confused," he said. "Confusion still has questions. These don't. They just stand there or walk aimlessly. No fight. No plea. No regret. They forget why they're here, like… ghouls."

"That's what Lethe does," I said. "It erases."

"Yes," he said. "But it used to erase the worst of their noise. The parts that made them unmanageable. This is… deeper. Wilder. It's not stopping where it should. We don't need more ghouls roaming." He hesitated. "And the mist is creeping."

I looked up sharply. "Creeping where?"

"Beyond its banks," he said. "Into the paths. And into Lethe Nomatos. It's thinning, but it's there. Guards stationed too close are coming back with gaps. Guards farther out are reporting… moments. Losing track of time. Of what they were doing. Some don't remember ever being angels at all."

"That's not possible," I said.

"It shouldn't be," he agreed. "But here we are."

Lethe Nomatos. The name sat heavily in my mind, like a stone dropped into deep water.

I'd discovered that secret part of Hell early on, back when I still thought obedience might buy me something, back when I was still naive enough to hope that if I did what He wanted down here, He might stop looking at me like I was the problem.

Azazael had been the test of that.

I didn't know he had gone to the First Light about me, and I didn't even remember what would make him or why. The memory lived blurred, like someone had smeared a thumb across wet paint—color with no lines. I knew only that it had been enough to make Heaven turn its head, to make Him look at me a second time, and somehow it made Him stamp traitor across Az's name and throw him out after me.

One moment, I had been alone walking through a cavern. The next, Azazael lay at my feet. Wings ripped to shreds. His grace was cracked and leaking. His face bloodied, and his eyes going in and out of focus, lucid just enough to understand exactly where he was. He stared at me like he was cataloguing… something, like the only thing that surprised him was that it had taken this long.

It was the one and only time I saw The First Light step into Hell, and He wasn't even really here. Not really. He smiled that smile and told me Az had come to Him about what I had done. His will pressed into my bones, bright and cold and absolute.

Contain him.

And Az... he didn't apologize. He didn't beg for his life. Not once. He just gave me twisted prophecies that made no sense.

I could have killed him. It would have been cleaner and honest in its own way. A single blow, a single choice, a single horror I could point to and say, "There, that's where I did it."

Instead, I did what I always did. I tried to please Him, tried to get in His good graces.

Lethe wasn't even half-formed, but in the shadows of a cavern, I found a hole, naturally carved from a cavern in bedrock and erasure, stone that sweated mist, walls that remembered nothing and reflected even less. It was a straight drop into silence at the bottom of a narrow chamber. And then I dragged a slab of rock over the top and piled it with loose stones.

They started calling it Lethe Nomatos, the place where even your name went to die.

I told myself it was mercy. That letting Azazael slip into unknowing was kinder than leaving him in the open to be used, twisted, and paraded as a living warning. I told myself I was sparing him.

He had looked at me before I dropped him in, not with hate. Not with forgiveness. Just recognition. Of what I was now. Of what I had been before. Like he understood that I was still trying to please the god who had thrown us both away, and that this was the shape obedience took now, down in the dark.

I pressed my thumb into my palm again until the phantom ache of Lilith's bite drowned under a different kind of pain, sharp and sour.

Now Lethe's mist was creeping where it shouldn't, into the paths. Into Lethe Nomatos. Into the place where I had left the only brother who had ever tried to stop my Fall.

Today wasn't the first time, I wondered if burying Az for Him had been the worst sin I had ever committed. And lately, the realm had begun to feel like it remembered that too.

First, Acheron is overfull and restless. Now, Lethe was hungry and leaking. Whoever was playing with my systems had a very specific sense of humor.

"Anyone fallen in?" I asked.

Sariel inclined his head. "Yes."

"Three demons," he continued. "One Lilin that tried to use the vapor as cover and stepped too far. It never resurfaced."

My jaw tightened. "The demons?"

"They resurfaced," Sariel said. "But they don't remember much farther back than two hours. One of them can't recall his own name. The other two remember only that they were afraid."

I exhaled slowly. "And?"

Sariel hesitated. "One Lethari."

That pulled my attention fully.

"It was cataloguing the bank," he added unnecessarily. "They know better."

"They all know better," I said.

Sariel's wings shifted faintly. "This one had been recording last thoughts. It stepped closer than usual. Witnesses say it paused… as if confused."

Of course it did.

"They say it looked at the water like it didn't recognize it."

"Did it resurface?" I asked.

"No."

Silence settled between us.

"They aren't prone to accidents," Sariel said carefully. "They inscribe warnings along the banks. They memorize the boundaries."

"And this one forgot," I said.

"Yes."

I closed my eyes for a moment, feeling the weight of it settle in my chest. Losing memories in Hell was normal. Necessary, even. Lethe existed, so eternity didn't drive every soul to immediate, screaming insanity.

But this wasn't that. This was erasure. Somewhere beneath that river, a Lethari was forgetting why it had ever been afraid of the water.

And then… something occurred to me.

"Was Lilith there?" I asked.

"No," he said. "She's been in the upper halls, last I sensed. Vespera's with her. They're…" His expression flickered. "…entertaining."

"Entertaining," I repeated.

The word settled badly, but it wasn't surprising. Lethe destabilizing. Acheron overfull. And Lilith was hosting salons in the upper halls.

I nodded once. "Has she shown any interest in Lethe?" I asked. "Before this?"

Sariel considered that. "Not directly," he said. "She's asked questions. But she asks questions about everything. About what each river does, what each structure costs. Nothing that stood out at the time."

Right. Nothing that would. Not unless you were already suspicious.

The bond pulsed, a low throb of satisfaction somewhere in the back of my chest. She was pleased with something. Or someone. Not me.

I turned away from him, pacing to the narrow window and back.

"What are you thinking?" Sariel asked.

That I'd let a spy sink her teeth into my neck and lace my power with hers. That my rivers were misbehaving like someone had given them alternate instructions. That the god who'd torn me out of Heaven had apparently decided the only way to feel safe was to hollow me out like a house he'd already condemned.

None of that was his question.

"I'm thinking," I said slowly, "that this isn't just accidental. Someone's testing how far they can push each system without snapping it."

"And next," Sariel said, "What? Styx? The Verge? The Garden?"

I was surprised she hadn't hit the Garden first. Or maybe she had, and I was unaware.

"Yes," I said. "If we let it."

He frowned. "You said 'someone.' Who?"

I looked at him.

Sariel had followed me out of Heaven when he didn't have to. Others had fallen because they'd chosen a side in a war they barely understood, or because I'd refused to apologize for a sin I didn't remember committing. Sariel could have stayed. He hadn't.

He'd walked beside me through fire and ruin and the kind of silence that only exists where music used to be. If there was anyone I could trust with the first cut into this mess, it was him.

The realization sat heavy and unwelcome. I didn't like needing help. I liked needing it from someone who'd seen me at my worst even less.

He waited, patient, the way he always did when he knew there was more.

"I need to tell you something," I said.

His brows lifted a fraction. "That doesn't sound fun."

"It's not," I said. "And it doesn't leave this room."

"Understood."

I hesitated anyway.

"This isn't like an order," I added. "This is… different."

He studied my face for a beat, then nodded once, slower. "Then I'll keep it like I keep my own," he said. "Or better."

The knot in my throat loosened a fraction as I sat on the edge of the desk because standing felt too exposed. Sariel remained where he was for a moment, then crossed the room and leaned his shoulder against the wall opposite. Just there, waiting.

"You know the bond," I said. "Between Lilith and me."

"I know you sealed your rule together," he said carefully. "Blood. Power. Matrimony. Everyone does."

"It was never marriage," I said. "In the beginning, it had felt like a braid, our power twisted together. But now, I've realized, it's more than that. It's a lattice. Her power threaded into mine. Mine into hers. It lets us anchor Hell more… efficiently."

"And that was the whole reason you did it," he said.

I huffed a humorless laugh. "No," I said. "The whole reason I did it was that I was newly cast out, newly crowned, and very fucking stupid."

His mouth twitched. "You're not the first to bind yourself to someone for the wrong reasons."

"I was lonely. It was… comfort," I said. "Solidarity. The illusion that if we were bound, we couldn't be turned against each other."

"And now," he said.

"Now I know she reports to Him," I said. "Directly. She's been using the pipeline I built. The Watchers. The rivers. She feeds Him observations about what I've built, what I've created here. And she keeps circling the same question," I continued, "whether what I built feels familiar."

I exhaled slowly.

"I don't know what she thinks I'm recalling. But it's not just her. It's Him, too."

Sariel went still.

"How do you know?" he asked quietly.

"The Watchers told me," I said. "Not in words. Through the tether. I caught Vespera messing with one, so I rerouted their messages. And then I heard one."

"And you're sure it was Him?"

"You've felt His attention before," I said. "You know what it tastes like."

He nodded once, reluctantly. "And you heard her?"

"I heard enough," I said. "She's been watching for cracks. In me. And I felt His fear. That I'll remember… something."

Silence settled between us again. Not empty. Heavy.

"But the bond," he said. "You think He's using it?"

"I think it was planned from the beginning," I said quietly, "He wanted to keep tabs on me, and she was sent to do that," I said. "This bond was a mistake. And I want it gone."

"You're going to break a blood bond with one of the oldest, angriest things in the universe," he said. "Quietly? Without alerting her? Or Him?"

"Yes."

"While she shares your throne?"

"Yes."

"And your bed?"

"Unfortunately."

"And your rule?

"For now."

He scrubbed a hand over his face, somewhere between horrified and impressed. "You really don't do small problems, do you?"

"If this were small, I'd have handled it already," I said.

He pushed off the wall and began to pace a short line of his own, thinking. "All right," he said. "Let's start with what you already know. How does a bond like that usually break?"

"Violently," I said. "Death. Or enough power forced through one side so that the other burns out. You can cut it, but it takes His hand to do it cleanly, and that's not going to happen."

"And you don't want to kill her?" he said.

"I've considered it, but…," I said. "I'm not sure if she can be killed. She seems pretty immortal. And… if it fails all at once, she screams. He hears. I lose the element of surprise. And Hell loses one of its anchors in the middle of whatever this is."

He nodded slowly. "So we treat it like we'd treat… a corrupted line," he said. "You don't rip it out while the system's live. You reroute.

You bleed it. You shift weight off it until it's just a thread. Then you cut that."

"That sounds nice," I said. "In theory. How?"

He looked at me for a long moment. "We start by finding where it's thickest," he said. "Where it carries the most. Then we give that load somewhere else to go."

"Somewhere else," I repeated. "Like what?"

His gaze flicked down, almost involuntarily, to my hands. "You've already built anchors," he said. "The rivers. The Garden. The Verge. The Choir. You said yourself they respond to you like they recognize your architecture. If we can deepen your connection to one of those enough, it might bear some of the strain the bond currently carries."

"You want me to offload part of my connection to her into Hell itself," I said.

"To your realm," he corrected. "To what's already yours. Right now, the bond is one of the main ways your power stabilizes this place. If we build a second pathway—another anchor just as strong—then cutting the first won't bring the whole thing down."

It was… not stupid. It was also dangerous as hell.

"It could twist the load," I said. "You know that. If I misjudge it, I tear the realm."

"You're already tearing yourself," he said. "Pick which failure you can live with."

Not many beings spoke to me like that anymore. I found that I didn't mind.

"And Lethe," I said. "Where does that fit in?"

He grimaced. "I was hoping you wouldn't ask that yet."

"Consider me greedy."

He sighed. "Lethe eats what's written," he said. "Memories. Names. The lines that say who you are and how you got here. If someone is tampering with it, they might be trying to soften you. To keep you from ever tripping over whatever He's afraid you'll find. Or they might be laying groundwork to... undo something already done."

"Such as," I asked.

"I don't know," he said. "And I don't love that I don't know."

"Join the club," I muttered.

He stepped closer to the bed, dropping his voice even though we were alone. "If Lethe's being pushed to erase deeper, and Lilith is reporting on what you do and don't remember, that seems more than just coincidence. That seems... deliberate. And... your bond is one of the main ways she knows what's happening in you... you can't leave it as it is."

I stared at him. "That was a very long path to 'you're right.'"

"I like to be thorough," he said. "You knew that when you dragged me out of Heaven."

"I didn't drag you," I said. "You jumped."

He smiled, briefly, without humor. "You're not the only one He underestimated," he said. "He thought I'd watch you fall and stay where I was put."

"And you didn't," I said.

"No," he said. "I didn't."

We'd never said it like that. Not plainly. We'd buried it under orders and banter and millennia of shared crisis. Something in my chest loosened and tightened at the same time.

"You shouldn't have come," I said quietly. "You could've stayed. Kept your halo. Kept His favor."

He snorted. "And spend eternity watching you burn from a distance," he said. "You're not that interesting, Lucifer."

"Liar."

"Occasionally," he said. "Not about this."

We looked at each other, the weight of everything unsaid stretching out between us like another tether.

"All right," he said finally. "So you want my help?"

"I wouldn't have said any of this if I didn't."

"Then here's what we do first," he said. "We go to Lethe. We see exactly how it's misbehaving. You fix what you can. And while we're there, we see if the river knows anything about what was taken from you before... everything."

I stared at him. "You want me to walk into the one place down there that exists to erase?"

"I want you to stand near it," he said. "I'm not suicidal. Neither are you. But you built Lethe. Even if you don't remember how you knew how, some part of you might recognize what's wrong. And if this... forgetting... is related to whatever He did to you before the Fall, we can't afford to guess from a distance anymore."

The idea made my skin crawl. I also couldn't argue with it.

"You realize," I said, "that if I misstep, I could lose more than a few hours."

"Yes," he said. "You could lose centuries. Millennia. Or yourself. Or... whatever He didn't want you to remember in the first place."

"Comforting."

"I'm not here to comfort you," he said. "I'm here to keep you from walking into it alone."

Something in the bond shivered, like Lilith had rolled over in her sleep. I felt a flicker of curiosity from her through the bond, but it faded quickly. She didn't know yet. But she could soon enough.

"Fine," I said. "We go to Lethe. We look. We fix what we can. And while we do, you start thinking about how to build a second anchor strong enough to let me cut the first one."

Sariel nodded. "I already am," he said. "And if we can use Lethe to our advantage along the way…"

I gave him a sharp look. "You want to use the river that eats memory as a tool to hide what we're doing."

"If we're very careful," he said. "And very lucky."

"Luck isn't a system," I said.

"No," he agreed. "But it makes a nice garnish."

Despite myself, my mouth twitched.

He straightened. "I'll get the path ready," he said. "Keep your distance from the mists until I say otherwise. And… Lucifer?"

"Yes."

"Don't tell Lilith you're going," he said. "Not until we know exactly how deep this rot runs."

"As if I would," I said.

He nodded once. "Then meet me later," he

said. "When the upper halls are quiet, in the throne room."

On the surface, that would look like nothing more than a late conference with my general. No one would question it. No one ever questioned me on that throne. And no one but the two of us knew about the passage I'd carved into the stone beneath it, a narrow stair that dropped under the dais and ran beyond the castle grounds, opening into a low underground chamber where five paths split, each one leading to the mouth of a different river.

"Fine," I said. "Throne room."

He slipped out, leaving me alone again with embers from the fire, the worn path in the stone, and the pulse of a bond I needed, finally, to break. Breaking it was going to take time. It would take planning. It might even take stepping closer to the one river in Hell I'd always avoided.

But for the first time since I'd let Lilith sink her teeth into me, I had something like a plan. The realization settled strangely in my chest, light and unfamiliar, like a muscle I hadn't used in centuries trying to remember its shape.

I wasn't reacting. I wasn't merely containing damage. I was choosing something for me, and I wasn't carrying it alone.

Something stirred beneath my ribs then—quiet, almost embarrassing in its softness. It wasn't defiance or anger. It was… hope. I almost rejected it on instinct. Hope had been burned out of me long ago, cautioned into silence by obedience and then exile and the slow rot of self-doubt.

But it was there. Small. Persistent. And for the first time in a very long while, I didn't immediately crush it.

CHAPTER TEN

Lucifer

The path to Lethe buckled under our feet. We weren't walking it, not really. Sariel was forcing it to cooperate. The corridor stretched, then folded in on itself like a serpent eating its own tail, stone rolling past us while he kept one hand on the wall and one on the hilt of his sword.

The sigils along his gauntlet flared faintly, and the rock responded in reluctant segments, distances compressing under his command.

"Hold," he muttered under his breath.

The hall kinked violently before straightening again.

"You're straining it," I said.

"It's resisting," he replied, "The mist from the Lethe is interfering."

There was another shift, and the stone rippled sideways, as if trying to spill us into a longer route. Sariel corrected it, dragging the geometry back into alignment with visible effort as his nose began to bleed.

Normally, watching the realm forced into submission would have amused me. Tonight, it felt like we were moving through something that didn't want us there.

Lethe's pull grew stronger with every turn, that low-pressure ache behind my eyes, a buzzing at the base of my skull. The air cooled, losing the dry heat of the upper levels, picking up that faint metallic chill I knew too well—memory, or rather the absence of it.

"You're quiet," Sariel said eventually, eyes forward.

"I asked you to drag me to a river that eats minds," I said. "Forgive me if I'm not in the mood for small talk."

He hummed. "That, and you're trying very hard not to think about why you really want to be here."

I shot him a look. "Careful."

"I'm serious," he said. "This is the one river you avoid like the plague, ever since you created it."

"Yes," I said. "Which is why you're coming with me."

The corridor finally opened, the ceiling dropping as we stepped into the throat of the cavern. Sound dulled immediately. The castle's distant roar faded to a hushed, slow drip of water, the low, constant hum of souls pressed too close together.

The river lay ahead like a strip of black glass cutting through the stone, its surface too still until you looked long enough to see what was crawling beneath. The mist clung low and thick, hugging the banks in a pale band that curled around ankles and knees like grasping hands when you got too close.

Tonight, it wasn't staying put.

Sariel wasn't exaggerating. Thin tendrils of mist had crept away from the river proper, spilling into the paths like fog that didn't quite know how to be fog. It reached up the walls in filaments, tasted the air, and pooled around the boots of the guards posted at the edge.

One of them blinked at us slowly, eyes unfocused. His jaw worked like he'd started a sentence and forgotten how it ended.

"Name," I said sharply.

He flinched, straightening. "M–Malkan," he said after a beat.

"How long have you been stationed here?"

His brow furrowed. "I… don't… know."

Sariel stepped forward, fingers brushing the mist. It recoiled from him, then slithered back, stubborn, like it recognized that we were trying to push it away and took offense.

"This started when?" I asked.

"A day. Maybe less." Sariel's voice stayed calm, but the knuckles on his sword hand were white. "It was hugging the bank at first. Now look."

He gestured.

The fog ghosted across the stone in veins, thinning as it went, but not stopping. It had already reached the side passage, a low, dark cut in the rock that led away from the main cavern.

The one that wasn't supposed to touch the river. The one that led to the pit where—

I cut the thought short. *Lethe Nomatos.* The place where even your name goes to die.

I stared at the tendrils creeping into that passage, and something cold slid down my spine. This didn't seem random.

"Containment?" I asked.

"We've tried," Sariel said. "Barriers bend around it. Fire burns through it, but it regrows from the river. It's not... natural, Lucifer. You made the river to strip memories, but this—this feels like searching."

"Searching for what?" I said.

His gaze flicked to me, steady, too knowing. "You tell me. It's your architecture."

I hated that word right then. *Architecture.* Like this was a palace and not a cage.

I stepped closer to the river. The mist thickened, curling around my boots, tasting the leather, the skin above. Instinct screamed to back away. I didn't. I crouched instead, watching how it moved, how it clung, how it didn't so much rise as reach.

Lethe moved differently from the others. While Acheron dragged grief and Styx bound oaths, Lethe was different. Lethe forgot. It ate edges first, then details. And then whole minds, leaving nothing but a frantic, gnawing hunger behind.

"Don't touch it," Sariel said under his breath.

"Please," I said. "Give me some credit."

The mist curled higher, brushing my wrist with something cold as knives. For a heartbeat, there was nothing. Then the whispers came.

It wasn't quite words. It was more... impressions crawling under my skin. Souls I'd thrown here for clawing at their own existence. Faces I'd turned away from. The sound of feathers burning. The smell of ozone and prayer.

Sariel's hand clamped onto my shoulder, fingers digging in. "Lucifer."

"I've got it," I ground out, forcing my thoughts to hold their shape, pushing the murmur back the way you push water off a stone. "It's testing. It doesn't usually test."

"That's what worries me," he said.

I shook my hand sharply. The mist peeled away, sulking back toward the river like a reprimanded animal.

Beyond us, the Watchers hovered in the shallows, not quite touching the river, not quite touching the shore. Just like the Watchers I'd made for Acheron, they were tall, long-limbed shapes wrapped in ragged black, gliding just above the ground like shadows that had forgotten how to lie flat.

But these were not silent constructs of suspension. The Acheron Watchers were mere anchors. They never formed words. They were built without them because the river did not require language. It required weight. Stillness. Pressure.

Lethe required something else. Memory. They lined the banks in a narrow row, holding the drifting souls in place, preventing them from wandering out of the mist before the forgetting finished its work.

They'd listened. They always did.

The ones closest to the encroaching vapor swayed faintly, their forms thinning at the edges. One turned its head toward us, slow as a rusted hinge.

"Master," he said.

His voice sounded like it had traveled through several lifetimes to reach his mouth. These Watchers had been given just enough mind and language to remember why they stood here.

"Yes," I said.

"I can't remember… why I'm holding," he said. "Only that I must."

The river hissed softly at that, a sound like steam through teeth. I bared my own.

"You hold because I said so," I snapped. "That's enough."

He bowed his head, accepting that as a new command, for now.

Sariel exhaled. "We need to know how far it's spread."

"We will," I said. "But first, I want to see the… shadow."

His mouth flattened. "Lucifer—"

"Don't," I warned. "You were there when I made it. Don't pretend you didn't approve."

"I was there after you obeyed," he said quietly. "Those aren't the same thing."

I didn't answer. I turned toward the side passage, toward the thin tongues of mist slipping into the dark like scouts. The stone under my boots changed with the first step. Smoother, more worn, like something had been pacing here for a very long time. The further we walked, the colder it got, the air heavy with an old rot that never fully bloomed.

Lethe's hum softened behind us, but it didn't disappear. It followed, low and persistent, tugging at the back of my mind, trying to catch something loose.

"You should've sealed this passage," Sariel said, low. "After you put him down there."

"I thought putting him there was sealing it," I said.

He didn't argue. That was worse.

The corridor bent once, twice, then opened into the chamber I'd found so long ago. It was small, covered in stones I'd left. Ten feet across with a low ceiling forcing me to duck. In the center, framed by a ring of darker stones, lay the heavy slab of stone.

Last time I'd stood over it, I'd dragged the rough stone over the hole. Now everything looked ancient. The stones had shifted as if something beneath them had pushed and failed. The slab itself sweated damp with spots of iron blooming orange rust.

Mist had seeped in here, too. Thin enough that it barely showed, but it clung to the stones on top of the slab like cobwebs, threads of forgetting reaching for what lay below.

I hated how much the sight of it made my stomach lurch. Lethe Nomatos. I'd done this back when I still thought obedience might buy me something like mercy. Back when I thought if I did His bidding, He'd forgive me.

I remembered how Azazael's face had been wild with warnings I refused to hear. After I'd left him and turned my back, I'd heard him once, knocking faintly on the underside of the stone slab. And I convinced myself it'd been the rock settling. But… I knew. I knew, walked away, and hated myself for it.

I left him alone in this place where memory itself rotted in the dark. And now the river that fed that oblivion wanted out.

Sariel crouched beside the ring of stones, hand hovering over the faint wisps of mist.

"It shouldn't be able to reach this far on its own," he said. "Not without invitation."

"Invitation?" I echoed.

"Something opened a door," he said. "Maybe not literally. But the river just doesn't decide to explore. It reflects what's poured into it. If its hunger is spreading, it's because someone deepened it. Pushed something into it."

"Who?" I asked, though I already knew the answers. The First Light. Lilith. Maybe both.

Sariel's jaw worked. "Who keeps asking you what you remember?"

Lilith's voice rose unbidden in my mind. *Are you sure you're not trying to recreate something?*

My skin crawled. I straightened, pressing my thumb into my palm until I felt the crescent of my own nail, anything to anchor me in the present.

"I didn't come down here just to admire my mistakes," I said.

"You want to use it," Sariel said. Not a question. "Whatever this is becoming. You want to aim it."

He knew me too well.

"I want to break something," I said. "Without her feeling it."

His eyes narrowed. "The braid."

The bond at my neck pulsed then, faint and smug, as if it liked being acknowledged. As if it liked being permanent.

"If Lethe can eat memory," I said, "can it eat pieces of a bond? Snip threads without severing the whole?"

"Lucifer…" His voice dropped, rougher. "That braid ties you together at the root. You try to cut it with this, you won't just singe a few strands. You'll risk hollowing both of you out. You could peel off entire parts of yourself and never know what you've lost."

"Would that be so bad?" I asked, too quickly.

His stare sharpened. "You don't mean that."

I didn't answer immediately. The truth sat heavily in my chest.

I couldn't do it anymore. I couldn't keep letting her in, not when she was sending pieces of me upward to a god who wanted to use me as a cautionary tale to further His own twisted agenda. I was no son to Him. I was a shadow to hide—a fracture in His perfect design.

You don't leave fractures unattended. You bind them. You watch them. You give them someone they think is just like them, and let them believe they're no longer alone.

I had let her close. Let her inside my pulse. My thoughts. My bed. My hands curled before I realized they had. The pressure around me tightened, as if Hell itself could feel the temperature rising in my blood.

I could still remember her mouth against my throat, slow and deliberate, testing the shape of what I was the way a scholar studies a rare language. Each pull of my blood had braided something of her into me, something cold and patient, until I could feel her presence threaded through my power like silk.

I had thought it was intimacy. I had thought it was recognition. Now I could see the design in everything. Every taste had been a measure. Every touch was a calculation. And I had opened the door for her myself.

And then a thought came to me. If I

couldn't break the bond without tearing myself in half… maybe I could make it lie. Blur it. Wrap it in something Lethe couldn't chew through. Or chew through the parts she used, leave the rest intact.

"I don't want oblivion," I said finally. "Not for me. Not even for her. I want… misdirection."

Sariel's brows rose. "You would be asking Lethe to forget selectively," Sariel said. "The river's never done that. It's not known for restraint."

"When you say it like that, it sounds reckless," I said.

"It is reckless."

"That's never stopped us before."

"Us," he echoed. "Is that what this is?"

"You followed me when you didn't have to," I said quietly. "You stayed. That makes you 'us' more than most."

Something softened at the edge of his mouth. "Flattery, now? You really are desperate."

The mist lapped at the dark stones on top of the slab, and I swear I heard a faint tapping forcing me to clench my jaw.

"If I do nothing," I said, "He keeps seeing through her eyes. She keeps digging. That river keeps spreading. Either it eats half of Hell, or I learn how to make it listen to me."

"And you think that starts with telling it to nibble on your blood bond?" he said.

"I think," I replied, "that if I'm the one who rules this cage, I should be the only one who decides what becomes of it."

Sariel stared at me for a long moment, like he was weighing every version of me he'd known against this one.

Finally, he said, "If we test this, we do it my way."

I lifted a brow. "Your way?"

"We start small," he said. "A lesser tether. Something that won't tear you apart if it snaps. We see what the mist does when we ask it to take only part and leave the whole. And if at any point it starts taking more than we offer, we pull you the fuck back."

"You're very certain you can pull me back," I said.

"You built the door," he said. "But I've learned how to move the walls. Between us, we can wrestle you out of your own mess one more time."

My throat tightened around something that wasn't quite gratitude and wasn't quite shame.

"Fine," I said. "We do it your way."

Sariel nodded once, decisive. "Then you need to find something you're willing to forget."

My mind flashed immediately to the feel of Lilith's teeth at my throat, her laugh in my bed, her fingers tangled with Vespera's in the shadows of my own halls.

"Willing is a strong word," I said.

"You want out of that braid?" he said. "You're going to have to sacrifice something it touches. That's how bonds work. You don't unmake them without losing something."

I looked down at the slab again, at the mist trying to creep under it. At the stones I'd stacked with my own hands around the friend I'd betrayed.

Once, I'd believed obedience was the cost of keeping a place in His story. Now… I wanted no place in it at all.

"I'll find something," I said.

Sariel straightened, stepping back from the slab. The mist recoiled from his boots, reluctantly.

"We'll need to clear the guards," he said. "Can't have anyone else catching stray pieces of you."

"Or of her," I added.

The thought made my stomach twist. Lilith didn't deserve mercy. But letting Lethe decide what parts of her to eat felt too close to what He'd already done to me.

I turned away from Lethe Nomatos, from that hole in the ground, from the ring of stones I'd once thought looked like closure and now recognized it for what it was—a monument to cowardice. My cowardice.

The mist followed us a few inches, then fell back, clinging to the stones like a dog chained to its yard. As we stepped back into the main cavern, the river's hum rose again around us, restless, hungry.

Sariel glanced at me. "So. Step one."

"Step one," I agreed.

Make the river listen. Teach oblivion how to lie. And hope, for once, that I could betray something other than myself.

CHAPTER ELEVEN

Lucifer

I waited until the right time, which didn't happen until weeks later, at night. When the castle finally quieted, it didn't go still. Hell never did. The noise just dropped a register, from roars and maniacal laughter and steel on stone to the softer sounds that lived underneath—whispered bargains. Choked moans of pleasure. Chains shifting when someone remembered where they were.

I waited until then.

Lilith was out, which helped. She'd gone to the Crimson Verge to "oversee drills," earlier in the day, which meant she wanted to watch people bleed for sport and pretend it was for discipline. Vespera had gone with her, of course. Two shadows moving in tandem down my halls.

Good. Let them stay busy somewhere else.

I left our rooms shortly after. I wore tight-fitting leathers and boots, my throwing dagger harness crossed over my chest, blades resting against my skin. I didn't need armor in my own halls. I was the thing other people needed it for.

No one asked where I was going. No one asked why. No one ever did. If anyone saw their king walking the corridors alone, they moved quickly.

The throne room loomed ahead, doors yawning wide, torches banked low. Only a few sentries remained—one at each pillar, another by the main doors. The rest had been dismissed for night rounds.

"Out," I said, without breaking stride.

They didn't argue. Their boots hit the stone, and then the room was mine. Sariel waited in the shadows off to the right, leaning against a column like he'd been born there.

"You're late," he said.

"I rule a realm," I replied. "I'm allowed to be late."

He pushed off the pillar and joined me at the base of the dais. "She ask where you were going?"

"No. She left with Vespera, never even noticing I was leaving."

That wasn't entirely true. Lilith always noticed. But she'd been too full of her own victories of late to care where I went.

We climbed the steps together. The throne sat in its usual place, carved out of dark stone, veins running through it, flecked with dull gold.

I sat for a moment, more habit than desire, fingers curling over the ends of the armrests. The bond pulsed faintly at my neck, as if it recognized the seat and wanted to preen. But I ignored it.

"Ready?" Sariel asked.

"No," I said. "But we're doing it anyway."

I shifted my weight, pressing my palm against a specific seam in the stone beside the throne. The mechanism wasn't mechanical. It was me. A command sank into the rock when I'd been in one of my more paranoid moods.

The dais shuddered faintly. Stone rearranged itself with a grinding sigh, and a narrow rectangle appeared beneath the throne, steps dropping away into darkness.

"After you," Sariel said.

"How generous," I replied as I descended first.

The air changed almost immediately, losing the faint heat of the hall. Down here, the air was more humid, denser, pressed close to the skin. The walls were smooth, carved by intention, not water. I'd made this tunnel when the rivers were still young, and I didn't trust any path that didn't answer directly to me.

The stairs turned twice, then emptied into the chamber I'd carved as a junction.

It wasn't large. Circular, ceiling low enough that the tallest demons had to duck. In the center, the floor dipped into a shallow bowl, and from its far edge, five archways opened, each one a throat leading into darkness.

Each arch carried a faint echo of its river. We moved toward the third one. It carried the edge of Lethe's chill, the hairs on my arms rising as I glanced toward it.

Sariel came to stand beside me, eyes moving from archway to archway.

"This is still impressive," he said.

"It's a way to get where I need to go without walking past everyone who thinks they're important," I said. "Impressive is an accident."

He huffed a quiet laugh. "And here I thought you liked showing off."

"Not for them."

I stepped toward the Lethe passage. The air got colder with each step, that familiar pressure building behind my nose, like I was about to walk into bright light, and my eyes were trying to flinch ahead of time.

Sariel followed.

"You could start with a different river," he

said. "Styx for oaths and bonds. It fits."

"Styx mostly binds," I said. "I don't need this tighter. I need it… confused."

"True," he muttered.

The passage sloped downward, stone underfoot slick with a thin sheen of condensation. As we walked, the faint, ever-present hum of Lethe grew louder under my skin.

"Did you find something you're willing to let go of?" Sariel asked.

I shrugged.

"Have you?"

I flexed my hands. The bond prickled, sensing I was thinking about it.

"There are a lot of nights with her I wouldn't mind losing," I said. "That seems like an easy start."

"It isn't," Sariel said. "You cut too close to desire, and you risk cutting the instincts that tell you who's dangerous. You'll start stepping toward her for all the wrong reasons, not knowing why. Or not stepping away when you should."

I grimaced. He wasn't wrong.

"Then what?" I said. "You want me to offer it my favorite color?"

He didn't smile. "Memories of something smaller. A lesser tether. Start with an anchor that matters, but not to you."

"Examples."

"Pick someone you've bound to you lightly," he said. "Not through blood. Through favor. Debt. A demon whose name you can still say without tasting iron."

I thought of the castle. The halls. The ones who moved when I told them to, just a fraction faster than fear demanded.

"Aluma," I said, before I could stop myself.

The gondolier, with her hollow eyes and her hands like bone hooks. The one who ferried souls across Acheron and never complained, even when they clawed at her wrists, trying to drag her in with them.

"She's tied to you through work," Sariel said slowly. "Through gratitude. Through the piece of yourself you gave her so she could stand in Acheron without being pulled under with the rest."

"Exactly," I said. "Which is why I hate this idea."

"Which is why it'll tell us something real," he countered. "We don't use the whole thread. Just a strand. Just enough to see how Lethe responds to being asked to nibble instead of devour."

We reached the end of the passage. There was no grand cavern here, no wide open space. This was a smaller mouth than the main approach. There was a side ledge overlooking a narrower arm of the river where mist clung thick and low, like a blanket dragged halfway off a bed.

Below us, the water was a black mirror, with the same crawling movement under the surface we had seen before. The Watchers lined this bank too, hovering just at the edge, their ragged black forms motionless.

They floated, bare inches above the stone, toes never quite touching the ground, as if gravity had given up on them. They didn't turn when we arrived. But I felt their attention like a shift in the air, a tightening along invisible threads.

"Master," one of them said. The voice came from nowhere and everywhere, as if the darkness where a face should be had swallowed the sound and decided to echo it back.

"Hold the line," I said automatically.

"We hold," it replied. "We do not remember why. But we hold."

And that was the whole point.

Sariel glanced at me. "You sure you want to do this here?"

"No," I said. "But we've already started."

He turned to face me fully. "All right," he said. "Call it."

I hesitated. Reaching for Aluma felt wrong,

like sticking my hand into the gears of something that had never failed me, to see if it would still turn. But I reached anyway.

The connection between us wasn't like the bond with Lilith. That one sat at my neck, braided through my veins, pulsing whenever she laughed or fed or lied. This one was deeper, lower. A knot in the center of my chest, tugging faintly every time I needed to call her to the bank of the Acheron.

I located it, where the bond lived. It was tight and threaded through muscle and memory. I pressed against it, mentally from the inside, applying pressure the way one might coax a splinter toward the skin.

It resisted, trying to twist away, but I persisted. Slowly and deliberately, I drew it upward, shifting it beneath the surface of my sternum until I could feel it just under the skin — a thin, heated line pulsing faintly against bone. Aluma stiffened somewhere downriver on Acheron. I felt that too.

"She's not going to like this," Sariel said quietly.

"She's not supposed to know," I replied.

I opened the sensation as I leaned over the river. Lethe's mist thickened as if scenting something vulnerable. It drifted closer, silver and whispering, drawn to the exposed thread beneath my skin.

"You're sure?" Sariel asked.

"No," I said. "But I've decided."

I focused on the precise point where the bond touched me. And I let the mist kiss it.

Cold sank through my flesh without breaking it. It wasn't painful. It was more like a numbness as absence was being introduced to presence. The fog curled tighter, curious, tasting the strand through my skin, testing which parts of it were memory and which were marrow.

I held there, just long enough.

And for a heartbeat, nothing else happened. Then I felt the tiniest… pinch. It wasn't like a severing or a snapping. It was more like something taking a careful bite.

Far away, along Acheron, Aluma's grip faltered. I saw it in my mind's eye the way I always did when I chose to look. Her bones tightened on the pole, and her knees dipped as the boat rocked under her. The soul in the hull lurched, tried to grab for her arm, and failed.

Her eyes lifted, hollow and furious.

"Lucifer," Sariel warned.

"I know," I said through my teeth.

Lethe tasted the strand, turning it over like a tongue tasting a new flavor. It wanted more. I felt that clearly. But it didn't yank.

"Enough," I said, voice low.

The mist hesitated.

I tightened my will. "Enough."

The fog peeled away from the strand and my chest bit by bit, reluctant, like it had been promised a feast and I'd handed it a crumb. That tether felt thinner now, frayed at the edge, but intact.

In the distance, Aluma steadied. The boat scraped the bank harder than usual. Somewhere, a soul yelped.

"She's going to refuse your call," Sariel said. "You know that, right?"

"She can," I said. "She's earned it."

He watched me for a moment. "How do you feel?"

"Cold," I said. "Annoyed. Still myself."

He lifted his chin toward the mist. "And it."

Lethe hummed under our feet, restless, but… listening. It had taken what I'd allowed. No more. Not this time.

"That's your proof," Sariel said. "It can be taught to portion. To take only what you give it."

I thought of the braid at my neck. Of the way the bond warmed whenever Lilith smiled at me like I was hers and not a project.

"Then the question," I said slowly, "is whether I'm willing to let it bite that close to the bone."

Sariel's gaze dropped to my neck, to the faint red mark where her teeth had first sunk in.

"You know exactly how far you've gone before."

"And your point?"

"If you're going to carve into your own bond," he said, "do it for your freedom this time. Not for Him. Not for her. Not for anyone, but yourself."

Mist curled lazily at the edge of the ledge, waiting.

I popped my neck, feeling the braid answer, sensing, perhaps, that I was thinking about it too much.

"Not tonight," I said.

Sariel's shoulders eased a fraction. "Good."

"Tonight," I added, "we taught the river a new trick. That's enough for one evening."

"For once, we agree."

We stood there a while longer, listening to the low hum of Lethe, the distant churn of the other rivers through the archways far above, and the soft, endless breathing of Hell.

Then we turned back toward the tunnel, toward the throne room and the lies waiting there. The bond pulsed once as I walked, curious. Almost fond.

"Enjoy it while you can," I thought, and

didn't let myself wonder which of us I meant.

CHAPTER TWELVE

Lucifer

By the time I decided to finally end it, weeks had passed. Weeks of testing the river. Weeks of letting Lethe nip at threads I could afford to lose. Old oaths. Minor favors. A half-remembered song that had nothing to do with Heaven and everything to do with a tavern in the Bronze Age.

And the last one was a war. A petty, unnecessary conflict in the mortal realm that I had justified as correction and balance.

Lilith had simply whispered, "They only kneel when they're afraid."

And I had done the rest. A suggestion here. A sharpened doubt there. I had poured temptation into men who were already thirsty for legacy and watched them mistake it for their own conviction.

Hell had gained hundreds of thousands of

souls from it. I told myself it was strategy and consequence. But now, I could see it for what it had been. A test. A proof of how easily I could be nudged.

As the mist curled higher around my skin, I let it linger. That one, I thought. That one can go. And after it was eaten out of the bond, I watched her, not openly. That would have been careless. But every conversation, every glance, every idle remark became a test.

I listened for hesitation. For curiosity. For the faintest indication that she felt the absence where that piece of us had once lived. But she never brought it up, and I never found it.

Lilith continued moving through the halls exactly as she always had—measured, amused, watching everyone else the way a predator watches water for ripples. If she sensed any erosion in the bond, she gave no sign of it. And that, in its own way, was worse. Because she noticed everything. Which meant one of two things—the river had worked perfectly... or she was letting me believe it had.

Either way, the clock had started, and I spent weeks pretending I wasn't biding my time and counting down to the end.

But that last night, when she lay beneath me, all fangs and soft skin, I was almost gentle. It wasn't fucking, but we weren't making love either.

I pushed deep into her, steady and relentless as her breath broke against my throat, and I felt her fang drag across my skin as her fingers dug crescents into my shoulders.

I moved like I always had with her, but slower, less cruel. I kissed her instead of just taking her mouth. Instead of wrapping a hand around her neck and squeezing while she came, my hands mapped her familiar lines like I was memorizing them, which was ironic, considering what I planned to do.

If she'd been paying attention, she might've noticed I was different. But she didn't.

When she came, she laughed, low and pleased, against my collarbone as she nipped it with her teeth, and pulled me with her. I let myself follow. Let myself be dragged under with the ecstasy, just this once, without biting it in half with suspicion.

Goodbye, I thought, as she went limp beneath me, breath evening out, but she didn't hear that part.

I rolled with her in my arms, and we lay tangled together for a while, her head on my chest, my fingers slowly stroking the curve of her spine. To anyone watching, it would've looked like affection. Maybe it was, in some warped way. Or maybe it was just habit.

Eventually, she shifted, looking up at me.

"I should go," she murmured, voice muffled against my skin.

"Urgent business?" I asked.

She laughed softly. "Something like that."

She slid away from me, cool skin slipping out of my hands, and rose from the bed. Black silk pooled around her feet before she pulled the slip up over her body, the fabric skimming her milky thighs, clinging to her hips. She never bothered with modesty.

"You don't need to wait up," she said, adjusting a strap. "I might be late."

"Wouldn't dream of it," I said.

She smirked at that, misreading my tone as indulgence.

At the door, she paused long enough to glance back, fangs just barely peeking as she smiled. "Try not to break anything while I'm gone, Lucy."

"You either," I replied.

Her laughter echoed down the hall as she left.

I listened from the bed as her footsteps turned right at the end of the corridor, not left toward the training yards or down toward the lower courts. I pulled on loose pants and slipped out to see her turn down the hall towards Vespera's rooms, which was no surprise.

I stepped behind a column, letting it blur

me as a shadow slipped out to meet her a moment later, horns catching the low light as Vespera leaned up and kissed her. They disappeared together around the bend, heads close, bodies brushing like gravity hadn't gotten the memo that they were separate people.

I hoped Vespera kept her distracted. It made what I was about to do feel less like betrayal and more like… balance.

I went back to my rooms and changed into leather pants and boots, buckled my dagger harness across my chest. Steel settled against my skin with familiar weight. I ran a hand over the faint scar at my neck where her teeth had first sunk in, the place where the bond felt loudest.

It hummed under my touch, smug.

The castle at this hour was all low light and long shadows, torches banked, distant sounds dulled. A few demons bowed as I passed. Others pretended not to see me, but they failed. No one stopped me.

The throne room doors stood half open. Sariel paced at the foot of the steps, hands clasped loosely behind his back, wings hidden, but the old posture was still there.

"Took your time," he said.

"I needed to say goodbye," I replied.

His gaze flicked to the mark on my neck,

then away. "Did she notice?"

"If she noticed anything, it was that she had somewhere better to be," I said dryly. "Come on."

I sent the guards away with a word. The room emptied without protest, echoes of their footsteps swallowed by the high ceiling. Alone again with stone and shadow and that damned throne.

I climbed the dais and sat down. Seconds later, the stone ground aside to reveal the narrow stair dropping away beneath the seat. Sariel followed me down.

"You've been avoiding this for weeks," he said as we descended. "For someone so determined, you're remarkably good at stalling."

"I've been testing," I corrected. "There's a difference."

"We've tested enough minor bonds to know it works," he said. "She didn't notice when you let it take some of those war memories. Lethe can take pieces without stripping the whole. So the only thing left is the part that actually matters, which is why, I'm guessing, you've suddenly rediscovered patience."

"I didn't bring you with me to pick apart my mind," I said.

"You didn't bring me at all," he replied. "I chose to follow you. To help you."

"Then your judgment is even worse than mine," I muttered.

The junction chamber opened around us, its five archways yawning like open mouths. The Lethe passage breathed cold up from its throat. I stepped toward it, but he stopped me as his hand closed around my forearm.

I looked down at it, then up at him, irritation already rising.

"Careful," I said. "Did you forget who you're grabbing?"

Sariel didn't release me. His grip stayed firm, steady, like he'd done this a thousand times before and knew exactly how far he could push.

"Yes," he said calmly. "And you're starting to forget who's keeping you from doing something stupid."

My gaze flicked toward the Lethe arch before I caught it. I rolled my shoulder under his hand, more to shake off the moment than the grip.

"Then you'd better make your point quickly," I said. "Before I decide to stop asking your advice."

"Before… we go down there," he said, "you should hear the rest of the plan."

"I thought the plan was 'feed the bond to the river and hope it listens,'" I said.

"Right," he said evenly. "Which is why I've

been working on an alternative to 'hope.'"

I stopped just inside the arch and turned to face him. "Tell me."

He studied me for a heartbeat, as if making sure I wasn't going to bolt. Then, he said, "You remember what I do with the halls? How I bend them? Shorten the paths. Pull distant rooms together when you don't feel like walking."

"Yes," I said. "And I'm grateful every time you spare me another lecture from a minor lord who thinks whining is a political strategy."

He ignored that.

"I don't only do it with stone," he said. "Paths are paths. Walls are just the easiest place to practice."

I frowned. "You're going to have to stop talking like a riddle."

"I can bend the way things connect," he said simply. "For a moment. The way power moves. The way one thing reaches another."

Understanding crept in, slow and unpleasant.

"You want to bend the bond," I said.

"Exactly," he said.

My eyes narrowed.

"Right now, it runs straight from her mark at your neck down into your core," he continued. "It carries memory, emotion. Every reaction she might want to taste."

"Yes," I said flatly. "I've noticed."

"If we let Lethe touch that path as it is," he went on, "the river will follow it inward. It will chew through everything connected to it. Including you."

"And you think you can stop that?"

"I can redirect it."

"How?"

"A loop," he said.

I stared at him.

"I fold the path at your neck," he said. "Just that section. The part where the bond sits closest to the surface. I bend it into a circle that runs just beneath your skin."

"So the bond feeds into itself," I said slowly.

"Yes."

"And Lethe eats the circle."

He nodded.

"The mist will find the loop first," he said. "It will follow it the way water follows a groove. The memories in that segment. The emotional charge. The pieces of you she's been feeding upward."

"And Lilith?"

"Shouldn't notice a thing," Sariel said calmly. "You've already proven that works. The river erased the memory of the war from the bond, and she never reacted."

I didn't argue with that.

"She'll feel the bond from your palms, and won't notice the change as it weakens gradually," he continued. "Less signal. Less heat. Less clarity. If she does, she'll assume distance or fatigue."

"And when the loop is gone? You can collapse it?"

"We could," Sariel said.

His tone made me look at him.

"We leave the one at your palm," he said. "Quiet. Harmless."

"Then," Sariel replied evenly, "When you're ready, Styx take it away."

Silence stretched between us.

"You've been thinking about this for a while," I said.

"Yes," he said.

"And you're certain it'll work?" I flicked my eyes his way.

"Mostly."

I studied the dark passage ahead, where Lethe's mist breathed slowly through the stone and let out a slow exhale through my nose.

"Fine," I said. "Let's do it." I arched an eyebrow and looked at him again, "But... if you snap something you can't put back, I'm throwing you in the river and telling everyone it was an accident."

"That's fair," he said.

We walked the rest of the way in silence.

The side cavern we'd used before yawned ahead, Lethe's lesser arm stretched below like a strip of obsidian black. Mist's fingers curled along the ledge, testing the stone. The Watchers lined the opposite bank, their ragged forms hovering above the ground, their hollow faces turned toward us.

"Master," one said, voice flat and distant.

"Hold," I told them.

"We hold," it replied. "We do not remember why."

"No one ever does down here," I muttered.

Sariel stepped close enough that I could feel his presence at my back, steady and infuriatingly calm.

"Face the river," he said quietly. "I need to see the mark."

I tipped my head to the side, baring the scar to the cold air. The skin there tingled as if it were already aware of what we were thinking about, as if the bond had ears.

Sariel lifted his hand, fingers hovering just over my throat, not quite touching.

"Tell me if this pulls too hard," he said.

"If I pass out, assume you've done

something wrong," I said tightly.

"Noted."

He closed his eyes.

Sariel's power didn't feel like mine. Mine tore and reshaped and commanded. His folded and smoothed. It took sharp things and curved them. I felt it now, like invisible hands pressing along the inside of me, tracing routes I hadn't known were routes.

The bond at my neck flared in protest, then instantly muffled, as if someone had put a hand over its mouth.

"There it is," he murmured. "Straight line from the neck."

"Lovely," I said. "Are you planning to rearrange my veins while you're there?"

"Hold still."

Pressure built at the base of my skull, then slid down, following the path of the bond. It reached the mark and pushed, not in, but... around.

The sensation was different. It wasn't painful, exactly, but it was wrong and disorienting, like stepping forward and finding the floor had become a wall. I gripped the edge of the stone ledge with both hands, knuckles whitening.

"Breathe," Sariel said.

"I am," I snapped.

It eased slightly.

"There," he said after a moment, voice strained with focus. "I've got it. The path is now looped. It's feeding back into itself instead of down. You might feel… doubled, for a bit."

"I already feel doubled," I muttered. "I've been living in someone else's story for ages."

"Ready?" he asked.

No, I thought. "Yes," I said as I made my way down to the bank.

"Step forward," Sariel said quietly. "Just enough to let the mist touch the mark. Nowhere else."

I swallowed. The urge to jerk away from the edge was instinctive and primal. Lethe did not forgive curiosity. Lethe did not forget what you let it taste.

I forced my body to move anyway. Cold kissed the bite. It wasn't the gradual chill of air or the soft curl of fog around your ankles. This was precise. A blade of frost pressed exactly where her teeth had been, the river's attention narrowing like an eye focusing on a single point.

"Hold," Sariel said, voice right at my ear now. "Don't fight it. Just don't follow it."

Great advice, I thought dimly, as Lethe's hunger latched on.

The loop tightened as Lethe tasted it. The

sensation was a hollow pressure, like something gently probing the scar of an old wound. I forced my breathing to stay even. Because if the bond carried my reaction, then she might suspect something.

The mist thickened around my neck. Then it bit. Cold slipped through the loop Sariel had made, sliding along the circle of the bond beneath my skin. Not tearing. Testing. Following the path like water in a carved channel.

For a heartbeat, an image flashed behind my eyes of Lilith's face above me, laughter on her lips, blood on her teeth. I locked my thoughts down hard. No fear or anger. Nothing sharp enough to travel the tether.

But then... I felt her. She wasn't near. She was somewhere far above in the halls of the castle. Feeding. The sensation surged down the bond like a pulse of heat—her teeth in someone's throat, the slow draw of blood, the dark pleasure she took in it.

For centuries, that feeling had been unavoidable. It had been shared. And now the rush of it slammed into my chest, rich and electric, like a predator's satisfaction.

I focused on that. On her. On the familiar rhythm of it. If she felt anything strange from me, anything abrupt, she would know. So I held steady.

I clenched my hands into fists as Lethe tasted deeper. The mist curled tighter around the loop, and the sensation shifted. The pleasure coming through the bond dulled slightly, like a voice heard through thickening walls.

I let a second rush of it rise through the bond the way it always had — the slow draw, the pulse of satisfaction, the dark velvet pleasure that came when she fed. It surged, sharp and electric, flooding my chest with heat that wasn't mine but had lived there long enough to feel indistinguishable.

I could almost taste it now. Iron and hunger and that quiet exhale she gave when she was pleased. It felt stronger than ever—bright and intoxicating. And for a heartbeat, I wondered if Lethe had sharpened the channel and stripped away any resistance, making her even clearer. Had I just allowed it to widen the path instead of hollowing it?

The surge crested almost painfully in its intensity, and for a terrifying instant, I thought the bond had resisted the river entirely. Still, I kept my expression neutral. My breathing evened, but inside, I felt it. Lethe had found the vein. And it had drunk deeper than she ever had.

"Hold it," Sariel murmured behind me. "Don't let it collapse."

"I'm holding," I said through my teeth.

But then, it thinned. That sudden… intensity collapsed in on itself. It rang like a bell struck too hard, clear, resonant, undeniable, and then—it faded. That warmth dimmed into an echo, and then a whisper. And even that began to slip.

The river worked quietly, gnawing through the threads of memory and emotion braided into that loop. Another pulse from her feeding reached me. Even weaker this time, distant, like a warmth remembered rather than felt.

I kept my breathing steady, my thoughts blank, giving her nothing that would betray what was happening. And far away, Lilith continued feeding, unaware that the river had already begun to hollow out the path between us. And with each passing moment, I could feel her less, the edges smearing and sliding away from the feeling like oil from water.

"Lucifer," Sariel said. "With me. Stay with me."

I clung to his voice, to the rough sound of it, to the way he always sounded faintly unimpressed even when the world was ending.

The river bit deeper. Heat flooded my neck, sharp and stinging. Then it went dead cold, like that piece of me had been dipped in snow and left there too long.

Something tugged. For a horrifying second, I felt the bond try to drag more of me into its loop out of habit. A reflex. A wounded thing trying to feed itself whatever it could reach.

"No," I snarled and shoved my will down, back toward my core. "You don't get anything else."

Lethe hissed, a sound only I could hear, like spittle forced between clenched teeth. The pressure built, tight and straining, and I felt the loop swell beneath my skin, the circle Sariel had bent glowing hot and overfull as the river gnawed through what it contained.

There was another memory frayed. Another pulse dimmed. And then—

There was a release as it drained. The tension didn't break. It just emptied. Whatever had been running through it was gone.

The mist recoiled slightly, as if disappointed there was nothing left to taste. It thinned, slipping back toward the river quietly. And I reached inward carefully.

The structure of the bond still existed. The anchor deeper in my chest that connected to my palm still held, and the corridor Sariel had folded had not collapsed. But the segment beneath my throat was vacant, like a conduit stripped bare.

Sariel exhaled slowly behind me. "It held,"

he murmured. "The loop's intact."

"Yes," I said, touching my throat. Intact and now empty.

And for the first time since she'd bitten me, there was no hum waiting beneath my skin there. No shared heartbeat.

There was a pause as I stepped back.

"Stay still," Sariel said quietly.

I felt his mind move again, not pushing this time, but easing. Releasing the pressure he'd been maintaining around the bend.

"I'm stabilizing it," he added.

The strange, doubled sensation inside me shifted — the faint echo of two paths occupying the same space resolving into one as it slowly settled.

Sariel drew the last thread of strain away carefully.

"There," he said. "The loop is gone."

For a moment, I swayed as disorientation took hold, but it slowly faded. I felt inwardly again—no hum, no tug. Just skin. It had been so long, and now I was just... me. Singular. Alone. I let out a shaky exhale that I pretended was a scoff.

"Well?" I asked, voice rough.

Sariel stepped around to face me, eyes searching mine. "Do you know who you are?"

"Pick a less philosophical question," I said.

"Do you remember her?" he clarified.

I pictured Lilith. The first time she'd walked into Hell. The way she'd offered that cut palm, eyes full of shared anger and a promise she'd never intended to keep.

"Unfortunately," I said. "Yes."

"Me?"

"You're the idiot who follows me around, bends paths, and talks too much."

He huffed. "Good. Then your memory's intact."

His gaze dropped to my neck. I reached for it without thought. The scar was still there, faintly raised, but the energy in it had gone silent.

"How does it feel?" he asked.

"Light," I said before I could think better of it. "And wrong. And… quieter."

He nodded, something like satisfaction flickering over his face.

"Then it worked," he said.

I straightened fully, rolling my shoulders, testing for hidden pain. There was soreness, yes. An ache under the skin where Lethe had gnawed. But nothing was missing where it shouldn't be. No blank spaces where memories used to live. Just an absence where she'd once been anchored.

The bond from the scar on my palm still pulsed faintly, distant now, like an echo coming through stone. We weren't severed entirely. Not yet. But the direct route she'd used, the vein she'd trusted, was gone.

"She'll feel that," I said.

"Maybe," Sariel agreed. "But she won't know what you did. Only that something is… quieter."

"Good," I said. "She can wonder."

We turned away from the river together, leaving the mist to curl and sulk along the edge of the banks.

As we walked back toward the passage, the weight on my shoulders didn't vanish. But for the first time since I'd let Lilith sink her teeth into my skin, it was a weight I could recognize as mine, and it wasn't braided with hers.

Not entirely.

The scar in my palm still pulsed faintly, a stubborn little echo buried under skin and spite. Harmless, I thought to myself, but I didn't believe in harmless things.

I flexed my hand once and knew I wouldn't leave even that much of her in me, not if I wanted to remind this place what belonged to me.

Sariel was quiet next to me.

"The rest of it," I said.

He glanced over. "What about it?"

I looked ahead at the torchlight bleeding across the stone. "I need her gone. Soon."

His expression didn't change, but I felt his attention sharpen. "I assumed as much."

"She built half her power in this place on the appearance of unity," I said. "On the idea that we were one force. One throne. One will. If I cut the last of it quietly, she'll feel it, but she'll hide the wound. She'll spin it. She'll make whispers do her work for her."

"You want to do it publicly?"

I smiled, though there was nothing warm in it. "Then there are no whispers. Only witnesses."

Sariel's jaw shifted. "Public means risk. She could—"

I cut him off, "Everything worth doing does."

He let out a soft breath through his nose, the closest he ever came to visible annoyance. "You're already thinking about the celebration."

Of course I was.

Ten thousand years in this place. Ten thousand years of Hell surviving me, fearing me, shaping itself around me. My reign.

Lilith had dragged the lower courts into preparing for months, dragging gold out of vaults, hanging old banners, polishing bones into ornaments, like that sort of thing impressed me. Every lord and leech in the kingdom would be there, dressed in silk and blood and ambition, all of them waiting to see what I would bless, what I would destroy, and hoping to see Lilith standing at my side when I did it.

Perfect.

"Yes," I said. "I'll give them a spectacle."

Sariel was silent for a few steps. "You want her humiliated."

I considered it.

"No," I said at last. "I want her erased from the narrative."

That, more than cruelty, was what made his eyes flick to me.

Down here, pain was common. Humiliation had become sport. But to stand before every creature in this kingdom of ruin and sever what they had all treated as sacred, useful, feared, and untouchable—that was not a lover's quarrel. That was revision. That was a conquest with an audience. And they'd never see it coming.

"She'll fight you," he said.

"I hope she does."

They wouldn't see the breaking of a bond. They would see a king surviving treachery. They would see me choose myself over the woman who had mistaken proximity for ownership.

The thought settled in me with chilling ease.

At the celebration, she would stand beside me as she always had, radiant and smug, expecting another performance of unity. Another display. Another night of blood and spectacle with both our names tangled together in the mouths of demons too frightened to say one without the other.

And then I would take her hand before all of Hell. I would let them think I meant to renew it. They would lean forward, hungering for it. And then I would tear the final thread out where everyone could see it die.

I could already picture the silence that would follow. The kind that only came when a room full of predators realized something larger than hunger had just entered it.

Sariel was still watching me. "Styx could do it. We can open the hidden passage, and you can call out the bond."

By the time we reached the stairs again, we had a plan, and the shape of it had settled fully in my mind. Not just an ending, but a correction. A blade drawn slowly enough for everyone to admire before it went in.

Ten thousand years. Let them come. Let them fill my hall and raise their cups and call us eternal. I would give them a show that would teach every creature in Hell exactly why even monsters bow to me.

CHAPTER THIRTEEN

Lucifer

Ten thousand years after my Fall, Hell dressed itself for a celebration.

Torches burned higher in the throne room, long tongues of flame licking up toward the vaulted ceiling. The flecked stone floor shone darker than usual, polished by a hundred lesser hands. Banners hung from the rafters, black and red and bone-white, stitched with my sigil as well as symbols of the rivers and the Crimson Verge, the Garden, the Choir. My work turned into heraldry.

They came for it, of course.

The highborn demons took their places along the tiers that circled the hall, all horns and armor and old power. The fallen gathered nearer the front, those who'd chosen exile with me rather than light with Him. Their wings were now blackened, but the fracture in their eyes was still familiar. River-bound creatures lingered in the shadows, too—one of Styx's marked men with chain brands on his wrists, Aluma near the doors like a shadow in a hood, a pair of Watchers hovering at the margins like torn silhouettes someone had pinned upright.

Closer still, the pleasure court lounged along the lower steps, all silk and teeth, succubi and incubi who'd seen more of my private life than I ever meant to show anyone.

The Lilin gathered closest to the throne, where the firelight turned their skin to shadow. They arranged themselves like art. Tall and long-limbed, their movements were slow, deliberate, almost languid. They were Lilith's… creations of sort.

And when their king entered, none of them looked surprised.

Still closer was a handful of mortal souls who'd sold their soul knelt in chains near the foot of the dais, brought in for judgment, their eyes wide with the kind of terror that made stories grow into fiction.

Sariel stood to my right, below the throne, plain in comparison, in gleaming golden armor and double-bladed swords at his back, his gaze steady.

Under the stone, beneath the dais, past the hidden stair, the nexus chamber waited. The rivers were listening. And the throne itself, the thing I'd finished carving out of dark stone and grudging authority, sat empty.

Trumpets sounded, low and rough, more growl than music. The murmurs in the hall rose, then dropped.

"Her majesty, Lilith," a herald called.

She knew how to enter a room.

Red silk poured through the doorway first, a slip dress that clung to her. It bared her pale shoulders and most of her breasts, fabric cut to hint and taunt. Her dark hair was loose, tumbling over her back. Her fangs showed in the smile she wore for the crowd, a flash of promise and threat.

At her side, a step behind and half-turned toward her, walked Vespera with her gleaming black horns curved back from her temples. Leather hugged her tall frame, and there was that strange shimmer in her presence that made lesser demons whisper *Nephilim* when they thought no one was listening.

They descended the central aisle together like they owned it. To be fair, I'd let them think they did.

I waited at the base of the dais, not seated. That got everyone's attention. Kings didn't stand for anyone here. I decided to let them wonder.

Lilith's eyes found mine as she approached, surprise flickering there for just a heartbeat before she smoothed it away into something pleased.

"My king," she purred, loud enough for the tiers to hear.

"My queen," I answered, letting the title ring off stone.

The court shifted, an exhale of satisfaction. They loved titles. They loved seeing them used.

I took her hand and brought it to my lips as if I were a patient man and not someone who'd spent months planning how to break what we'd built. Her skin was cool. The bond that still ran between us at the palm pulsed, curious and smug.

"Walk with me," I said.

I led her up the steps to the throne. She moved easily beside me, her gown whispering around her legs, the scent of old salt and older hunger clinging to her. Vespera watched from below, eyes narrowed, hands clasped behind her back like a soldier on parade, except for the way her shoulders tilted toward Lilith even now.

We turned at the top to face them all. Hell's court stared back, expectant.

"Ten thousand years," I said, my voice carrying without effort. "Ten thousand years since I Fell, and they named me adversary. Ten thousand years since Hell was given to me as a sentence, and I made it a kingdom instead."

A ripple of sound moved through the hall, not quite applause, not quite a growl. Something approving. Something hungry.

I let my gaze pass over them slowly, the lords at the edges, the chained souls at the front, the river's servants, the Watchers' empty hollows, Vespera's sharp profile. Last, I looked down at Sariel.

He gave the tiniest nod before I looked back at the court.

"In that time," I went on, "this realm has burned, broken, held, and rebuilt. The rivers ran. The Garden remembered. The Verge bled. The Choir hummed." I spread my hands slightly. "Hell stood."

"And so did we," Lilith said smoothly, stepping a half pace forward, letting the crowd see her clearly at my side. "Your king didn't rule alone. He never did."

And… there it was. I turned my head, gave her a look that could be read as fondness. Let them see what they wanted to see for a moment longer.

"You're right," I said. "I didn't. When I first took this throne, it tried to crush me. When I first laid the rivers, they tried to drown me.

When I first bound this realm to my will, it tried to split me in half."

Soft laughter rose at that, the kind that tasted like recognition.

"I might've let it," I said, "if I'd had to carry it alone. But I didn't."

I took Lilith's hand again and raised it for all to see.

"She came to me bloodied and cast out," I said. "Rejected by Eden as I was rejected by Heaven. She stood beside me, encouraging me, while I dragged order out of chaos and carved the borders that kept this place from eating itself alive."

I felt her preen at that, just enough to slacken her caution.

"You all know her as queen," I said. "You've seen her teeth. You've seen her mercy when it amused her. You've seen her rage when it didn't."

A few unfortunate souls shifted at that. They'd seen more than that.

"What many of you haven't seen," I continued, letting my voice soften just slightly, "is how we first bound this place. How we bound ourselves to it, and to each other."

Lilith's gaze flicked up to me, something like nostalgia in it. "Lucy—"

I didn't let her finish.

"Ten thousand years of rule," I said, louder. "Tonight, we will renew the pact that steadied Hell. The blood that anchored it. The oath that kept it from tearing itself apart."

Murmurs rose, excited now. The highborn leaned forward. The servants of the rivers straightened. Even the Watchers seemed to lean in, their hollow faces tilting toward us.

I turned to Lilith.

"Do you remember?" I asked, pitched low enough that the court had to strain to hear. "The first time we stood here and split our palms. 'Hell needs two anchors,' you told me. 'Two wounds in the world that never healed.'"

Her smile deepened, sharp and satisfied. "I remember," she said. "We bled for this throne. For each other."

Yes, I thought. You did. I let my fingers slide from hers and lifted my right hand. A lesser demon scurried forward to offer the ceremonial blade, hilt out, eyes down. I took it.

The steel gleamed dark, the edge soaked in a hundred old oaths. Beneath us and through us, Styx listened.

I turned my palm up to the hall. "You witness," I said. "All of you. You'll see what held you when the lies above you shifted like sand."

They hushed as I drew the blade across my

palm. Pain flared, bright and familiar. Blood welled quickly, dark and thick, dripping over my wrist.

I didn't heal it. I handed the blade to Lilith.

She took it with a flourish, eyes shining, and held her own hand up.

"For ten thousand years, they called you adversary," she said to the hall. "They forgot that to stand against Him, someone had to stand with you."

She cut her palm without flinching. Pale skin parted, and a deep red rose to the surface, running over her slender fingers like a lover as she turned back to me.

"Let them see, my king," she murmured.

I offered my hand. Our palms met, bloody skin to bloody skin, fingers lacing, the old scar between them flaring to life as it had only been sleeping all those years.

The bond roared. Not the faint hum I'd grown used to at my palm, not the muted echo after Lethe had chewed through the neck mark. This was the core of it, the place where we'd first braided power and consequence together. It surged up my arm, greedy and relieved, as if it had been waiting for this.

Under the throne, deep in the stone, I felt Sariel move. Not his body, but his will. The paths bent, not in the walls this time, but in bright, invisible lines tying my hand to the nexus below.

The rivers shifted. Acheron dragged its attention toward us like a chain scraping rock. Styx coiled tighter, scenting a vow. Lethe shivered, remembering the lesson it had learned.

I held Lilith's gaze as our hands squeezed.

"By Acheron," I said, my voice low and steady, "by every grief this realm had swallowed and every loss it refused to forget."

The air thickened, heavy with the weight of a thousand unburied sorrows.

"By Styx," I went on, "by every oath sworn in this place and every punishment for those who broke them."

Somewhere along the wall, the chain-marked envoy shuddered.

"By every river that ran through Hell," I said, "and every soul they'd carried, I call this pact to account."

Lilith blinked.

"Lucifer," she began, a warning in it now as she began to lift her palm away.

I tightened my grip.

"When we first bound ourselves," I said, still for the hall, for her, for the thing listening under our feet, "we swore to anchor this realm together. Two wounds in the world. Equals. Shared power. Shared consequence. No secrets that could break the stone we stood on."

Silence pressed in. I let it stretch just long enough for every demon in the room to taste it.

"And yet," I said quietly, "there were secrets."

Lilith's fingers twitched in mine. "This wasn't—"

"Watch him and tell me if he remembers," I said, and the words were no longer soft.

The hall went very, very still. Lilith froze.

"That was the charge, wasn't it?" I asked. "When He sent you down. When He wrapped you in your own rejection and promised you a shard of my throne if you sold Him every crack you saw."

Her mouth parted. No sound came out.

"You told Him when I dreamed," I said, each word crisp and clean as a blade. "When I shaped. When I walked in the Garden. When I built a place for grief that didn't fit His story. You asked me what I remembered, again and again, until the question itself stank of Him."

Vespera shifted below us, a step forward she didn't seem aware she'd taken. Her eyes were wide now, fixed on Lilith's face.

I kept my hand clamped around Lilith's. The bond strained, suddenly unsure where it wanted to run.

"I bound myself to you," I said, "thinking we were two sides of the same coin. Two exiles, rejected by the same hand. I thought you were here because you had nowhere else to go." I leaned closer, my voice dropping. "I didn't realize you were still working for Him."

Color drained from her cheeks, leaving her pallor more corpse-like than seductive.

"You don't know what you're saying," she hissed, barely moving her lips. "You're speaking madness in front of all of them."

"Am I?" I asked. "Then they can watch madness work."

I looked up, past her shoulder, to the gallery where the fallen stood.

"You saw it," I said to them. "All of you. The questions. The way she passed information to her new pet through the rivers. The way she sent my own creations upward as nets. She didn't just share this throne. She reported on it."

Vespera flinched like I'd struck her.

"Lilith of Eden," I rang out, letting her old title cut. "Lilith, first wife. Lilith, mother of demons. Lilith, spy."

The word dropped into the room like a stone into still water.

The bond at our palms convulsed. Under the throne, Styx surged. This was the river's true nature, the one anyone hesitated to wake.

It rose through the stone like a dark pulse, rushing up the hidden passage, onto the dais. It wrapped around my feet, my legs, my spine, my arm, my hand. It wrapped around the blood between our palms.

Heat hit first, searing where our skin met. The mixed blood turned hot, then hotter, then something beyond heat, like molten iron trying to remember what it felt like to be water.

Lilith gasped, eyes widening.

"What are you doing?" she whispered, voice fracturing.

"Calling in a debt," I said. "This pact was made on the understanding that you stood with me. That your loyalty lies here, not above. You broke that before the blood ever dried. Styx doesn't kindly overlook oathbreakers."

She tried to jerk her hand back. I held it tighter.

"You can't do this," she snapped, voice rising. "You need me. This realm needs—"

"It needed an anchor that wasn't nailed to His throne," I said.

The blood between our palms darkened, veins of black threading through the red. Light flickered around our joined hands, thin and sharp, outlining something that hadn't been visible in ten thousand years—the braid of the bond itself, shining under our skin where it crossed from my flesh to hers.

It tightened. Then it began to fray.

Lilith screamed. Not in fear, but in rage. Her fangs snapped down fully, her other hand clawing at my wrist.

"Lucifer," she shrieked. "Think. If you do this, you'll be alone. You'll have no shield, no second anchor, no one to stand between you and Him when He turns His eyes back to you."

"He already did," I said. "He sent you."

The braid burned as pain lanced up my arm, bright and brutal. I gritted my teeth and let it come, refusing to pull away. My half of the power, the part of me I'd bled into her ten thousand years ago, flared and tore itself free of the shared strand, snapping back into me like a dragged chain.

On hers, the bond didn't come home. It ripped.

Her palm blackened along the line of the old scar, the flesh splitting, light and shadow pouring out of it in messy, violent bursts. Power yanked out of her, not toward me, but down, through the stone, into the waiting throat of Styx.

Payment, long overdue.

She sagged, knees buckling. Only our joined hands kept her upright. And I let her hang there a moment.

"Look at them," I said quietly, nodding toward the hall.

Demons stared, rapt, at the spectacle of a queen brought low. The fallen watched with something like grim understanding. The river's servants had gone very, very still.

Vespera's face had collapsed around her eyes. Shock, betrayal, and something like animal panic warred there.

"They'll carry this story," I said to Lilith. "They'll tell it exactly as they saw it—their queen named spy and oathbreaker. Her blood pact unmade. Her power stripped as penalty."

She fought for breath, lips peeling back from her teeth. "You think this will change His story?" she rasped. "You think they won't twist it into proof that you were always everything He said you were?"

"Maybe," I said. "But they won't forget why I threw you out."

Her gaze flashed with pure hatred then, something cold and sharp and terribly familiar.

"You'll regret this," she whispered. "Someday, when whatever you lost tries to find you again, and it can't, you'll come crawling back and beg me."

Something in my chest twisted, hard. That

old, nameless grief rattled its chains. I refused to let it speak.

"Lilith," I said, letting my voice carry one last time. "By the rivers of Hell, by this throne, by the blood we once shared and the oath you broke, I strip you of the title of queen. I sever what remains of our bond. And by my dominion over earth, He thought was a consolation prize, I cast you back to the dust He denied you."

The last threads of the braid snapped then, with a sound only I seemed to hear, like the crack of something very old breaking along a fault line, and our hands tore apart.

Lilith staggered backward, clutching her ruined palm to her chest. Her dress, so carefully chosen, was spattered with her own dark blood.

Then, the ground answered me. The dais shuddered. Cracks spidered out from where we stood, racing toward the center of the hall. The mortal souls screamed. Demons grabbed for anything that looked solid.

Directly beneath Lilith's feet, the stone gave way, not into fire or a river, but into a tear that wasn't quite shadow or light, a raw wound that opened onto somewhere far, far away. I caught a glimpse of dry earth and hot sun, a horizon that wasn't this realm's. Sand. Rock. A mortal sky.

Her eyes met mine one last time, wide and furious and afraid.

"You'll be alone," she said again, but this time it sounded less like a threat and more like a curse.

"I'd been alone since before I Fell," I said. "I just finally stopped pretending you changed that."

The tear yawned wider. She dropped, red silk rippling in the wind, and the rift snapped shut behind her, leaving only the faintest scorch mark on the stone where she'd stood. The bond in my palm went silent. It was gone.

The throne room held its breath.

Then everything erupted at once. Demons shouted. Some roared approval, others outrage. The chained souls sobbed. The servants of the rivers bowed their heads. One of the fallen laughed once, a broken sound he choked off quickly.

And Vespera… we locked eyes. She didn't scream. She didn't charge me. She just went very, very still, then turned on her heel and ran.

She bolted down the central aisle, her horns catching torchlight one last time. Guards reached for her and thought better of it. Sariel took a step like he might intercept her, then stopped, eyes tracking her instead.

She didn't look back. She fled. Fled the

castle, fled the realm, fled whatever she'd thought she'd found in Lilith's shadow. Whether she ran toward Earth, toward Heaven, or into the cracks between, I didn't know, or care. I only knew she ran from me.

"Enough," I said, and the word came out cold as Lethe.

The noise cut off bit by bit, like strings being severed.

"This is what happens," I said to the hall, "to those who stand at my side with their faces turned upward. Hell does not have room for anyone else's gods."

I didn't wait for questions. I didn't invite them.

"Court is dismissed," I finished.

They all scattered, including the Lilin. Some bowed deeply before they fled. Others left without meeting my eyes. The Watchers drifted back into their shadows. The chain-marked envoy of Styx slipped away quietly, as if satisfied.

Sariel climbed the steps to me, searching my face. "It's done," he said.

"Yes," I replied.

"Did you—"

"Not now," I said, and even I barely recognized my own voice.

He studied me a heartbeat longer, then nodded and stepped back.

When the last of them were gone, and the torches in the throne room had dimmed back to their usual sullen glow, I left without looking again at the scorch mark where she'd stood.

The passage under the dais waited. The nexus thrummed. The rivers whispered my name. But I ignored all of it. I went to The Garden of the Forsaken… my Garden. I didn't know what I was searching for there. Only that I couldn't stop going back.

Thank you so much for reading Throne of Ashes, the prequel to the Hell of a Time dark romantasy series.

I hope you enjoyed it! If you did...

Help other people find this book by writing a Goodreads review.

Sign up for my email list so you can know when the next book is coming out.

Come follow me on Instagram, TikTok, or Facebook.

Use the QR code below to visit my website:

Sneek Peak
Chapter 1 of The First Sin
Lucifer

Hell was quiet tonight. There's always screaming somewhere down here, even if it was distant and well-earned. But this wasn't that. It was too quiet. Strange quiet. Odd quiet. This was the kind that hums beneath the surface, like it was anticipating and just wrong.

I was in bed. Three women tangled in my sheets. One riding me, slow and steady, chasing her own pleasure. The other two were too wrapped up in each other to notice anything else.

I let it happen. Let my body do what it was made to do, even if I felt nothing. I came inside her with a sigh, detached and inevitable, and only then did I look up.

The temperature had dropped. Not by much. Just enough to make the candles shudder. Just enough to know she was here.

Lilith.

She stood at the edge of the bed, in red silk and shadow, like she'd never left, like the fire in her had never gone out.

"Well," she said, her voice dripping in velvet. "I see you've kept busy."

I didn't answer right away. I watched the smoke ripple from the candle nearest her. Watched how even Hell's flames hesitated around her. Then I glanced at the women. None of them noticed or cared that she was here.

"Not busy enough, apparently," I muttered, brushing the woman off me as I sat up. "What do you want, Lilith?"

She pouted. "No welcome kiss? No clever insult? No gloat that I've finally crawled back to you?"

"You'd never crawl, and I assumed you wanted something," I said, swinging my legs off the bed and reaching for my robe. "And you never come just to reminisce."

I flicked my eyes to her. She moved like a flame—lazy, lethal, inevitable. She perched at the foot of the bed, careful not to touch the women. "I come with news."

"I'm not interested."

"You should be."

I stood. Towered over her. She smiled wider.

"Daddy's little plan needs... accelerating," she said. "And since you've been... distracted—" her eyes flicked to the bed, "I've taken the liberty of moving things along."

"What things?"

She rose and crossed the room to me in two steps, close enough that I could smell the smoke under her perfume.

Close enough to remember how she once dragged me into another rebellion with a single whisper.

"The Apocalypse, darling," she said, cupping my cheek mockingly. "It's time to get the show started."

I caught her wrist in one hand and let the other settle at her throat, not to squeeze, not yet, just enough to remind her how easily the world could stop if I wanted it to. I leaned in close, close enough to taste iron on her breath, close enough for her to understand that mercy, in that moment, was a choice I was still making.

"You don't give the orders," I said. My thumb dug a little into the pulse under her jaw. The pressure was casual but absolute. "I do."

She laughed, brittle. "I do when I have your crown."

She thought she'd won. Her grin sharpened, a hint of fang showing. She smoothed her dress as if I hadn't just put her life in the balance.

"I've taken your throne," she said breezily. "Hell is mine now. And you? You're going on a little field trip."

"Really?" I laughed, bitter. "For what? A soul harvest? A plague?"

"To fuck someone," she said sweetly.

I let the air out between my teeth. "What?"

"You heard me." She plucked an apple from thin air, polished it on her hip, and took a bite. "You're going to find the mortal girl, get her to fall in love with you—without using your magic, glamours, or that... voice of yours, and plant the seed."

Something about the way she said "mortal girl" snagged under my ribs, but I let it go. I stared at her. "And if I don't?"

"Then I do it myself," she said, smile gone cold. "But you know how messy I can get."

I didn't move. She stepped back into a ripple of flame and gold, already halfway gone.

"Oh," she added, eyes glowing now. "One more thing, my love..."

"What?"

"If you fall for her? You lose. Everything."

A blink later, she was gone. Vanished.

And for the first time in a millennium, Hell felt colder than Heaven ever did.

The next morning, I woke alone. After Lilith had gone, it only took a few moments before I was transported back to my second home, my old digs—the penthouse in Las Vegas.

Silk sheets clung to my legs, warm with the remnants of last night. A half-empty glass of something expensive perched on the nightstand. I picked it up and took a long drink, its contents flat and too sweet. Perfume still lingered in the air, cloying and unremarkable, left behind by someone whose name I hadn't bothered to learn.

The place gleamed around me in gold and glass, untouched by time or consequence. Floor-to-ceiling windows opened to a desert skyline lit up like a hallucination—Vegas pretending to be heaven, as usual. Glittering. Gritty. Gorgeous, if you squinted. It should have been enough. It used to be. But this wasn't a throne. This was a cage.

I hadn't built The Revel. I'd taken it years ago, ripped it from the hands of a mortal who thought he could game the House and outwit Hell. Outwit me. He lost. They always do. Now he had no name, no legacy, no soul. And I had a tower.

I rewrote the records, changed the deeds, gutted the bones of the place, and rebuilt it floor by floor until it gleamed like the Pyramid of Khafre eons ago. The Revel was a pleasure palace—a monument to indulgence, and the perfect place for my earthly kingdom.

But now? It was my prison.

Lilith had stripped the fire from its bones and sealed the doors to the underworld with the kind of magic only she could wield, given to her by The First Light. She'd left me stranded here in mortal skin, ruled by mortal rules, with nothing but time and the taste of ash in my mouth.

She let me keep this kingdom. Because she knew the truth—I didn't have dominion anymore. Sure, I owned the building. But not the rules. Not the world. Not even myself. And this gilded cage of gold and sin was all I had left.

I reached for the phone on the nightstand and pressed the single button I kept programmed. It rang twice.

"Yes, sir?" Topher answered, his voice smooth as smoke and just as thin.

"Stock the penthouse," I said, my voice still rough from sleep and smoke and something worse. "Bar. Kitchen. Closet."

A pause. "Sir?"

"I'm staying," I said, rolling my neck as I stared at the view. Vegas bled heat into the horizon. Neon simmered in the bones of the city. "For a while."

Topher exhaled, as if he knew what that meant. "Yes, sir. I'll make the arrangements."

"And send someone to deep clean," I added. "I don't want to smell last night on anything."

"Of course, sir."

I didn't say goodbye. I never did.

I moved like a man not in a hurry, but with nowhere else to be. Black slacks. Shirt unbuttoned to my sternum. No tie. No need. I was the reason rules were bent in the first place. I stepped into the elevator, its polished gold accents gleaming like teeth. The Revel was a sanctuary of excess dressed in velvet. If I had to be caged, I could do it in a palace built on sin.

The elevator opened to chaos. Slot machines screamed and blinked. Laughter rang brittle from the lips of losers. Glasses clinked over games no one ever really won—the air stank of hope and regret.

I moved through it like a shadow. My usual haunt was The Serpent's Tongue, but I didn't stop there. I wasn't in the mood for real. Not tonight. Instead, I slipped into one of the flashier bars— glossy, loud, neon-bright. Ecliptica, a two-level dance club that was easy to get lost in. Soulless. Perfect.

I took a seat at the edge of the action, ordered something overpriced and pointless, and waited. The night always came to me. It didn't take long. A blonde in a backless dress. A man with a sharp jaw and sharper intentions. Another woman, a redhead, younger, already glassy-eyed and aching to forget. They drifted toward me like moths that didn't care about getting too close to the flame.

Flirting. Laughing. Touching. I let them. Men, women, both—it didn't matter. If they were willing, they'd do. Desire was still allowed. Pleasure was still currency. And short-lived indulgence was still better than silence and my own thoughts.

They followed me without question. The man was cocky, in his late twenties, and liked being watched. The blonde was chewing gum and laughing too hard at nothing. The redhead, she was already tipsy, already dreaming. It wouldn't mean anything. Not to me.

The elevator ride was silent. The man adjusted his collar like he was about to step into a scene he'd imagined since he was fifteen. One of the women whispered about the suite to the other. About how "insane" it was that I lived here.

I didn't answer.

The penthouse doors opened. Lights rose. The skyline blinked like a mirage.

"Jesus," the blonde breathed, spinning slowly. "Are you, like... royalty or something?"

I smiled, thin as a blade. "Close."

I shrugged off my jacket, tossing it on a chair. Unbuttoned my cuffs. Poured four drinks. Handed them out like communion. They looked to me for direction. Permission to want. Permission to unravel.

I stepped closer to the man first—just enough to make him freeze, then lean. Then the redhead kissed me. Her lipstick smeared, but she didn't care. The blonde giggled, dropped her purse, unzipped her dress, and let it fall to the floor.

They stumbled toward the bedroom like sinners chasing something holy, drunk on the idea that I could absolve them. And maybe I could. So I followed. Not because I wanted them. But because they didn't matter.

If I didn't care, it couldn't touch me. If it meant nothing, it couldn't crack me open. If it was just skin and heat and noise, maybe that was enough to keep the silence out. So I fucked them like a man with something to bury. Not love. Not memory. Just the echo of a crown I no longer wore.

No tricks. No power. Just fingers digging into flesh. Mouths pressed to sweat-slick skin. Teeth and lips and bodies that didn't know they were standing in a graveyard.

The bed creaked under it. The walls held it. The air tasted like smoke and want and something sweet and half-rotten. And still, I didn't feel a thing. Not even when they moaned my name like it meant something. Not even when they begged, because this wasn't desire, it was punishment. And I gave it to them the way only a fallen angel could. Ruthless. Beautiful. Empty.

Each one collapsed, spent, into my sheets. I lay awake, staring at the ceiling. Alone, even with three warm bodies beside me.

When dawn began to smear light across the skyline, all I could think was, "She's out there somewhere. And if Lilith is right—"

I didn't finish the thought. Instead, I climbed out of bed, stepped over the man's shirt, and poured myself a drink.

Morning came with no mercy. I stood at the window, shirtless. Cigarette between two fingers. A glass of warm scotch in the other. My pants hung low on my hips, zipper half-undone, like even my clothes couldn't be bothered to finish.

Behind me, the bed was a snarl of limbs and silk. The blonde snored, her leg draped over the man like she'd claimed him. The redhead had rolled onto her back. A bruise bloomed at her collarbone, just above the imprint of my teeth.

I didn't know their names. Didn't want to.

The city sprawled beneath me, painted in neon and sin. It used to thrill me. Now it just looked cheap.

I heard the click of the private door.

Topher entered without fanfare, two black shopping bags in one hand, a leather case in the other. His presence never made a sound.

"I brought what you asked for," he said, crossing to the counter. "Liquor. Clothes. The kitchen will be restocked within the hour. Fresh towels."

I took a drag from the cigarette. "I burned the last ones."

"Yes," he said evenly. "Spectacularly."

I turned slightly, just enough to catch the twisted sheets and tangled bodies in my peripheral.

"Get these humans out," I said, voice flat. "Quietly."

"Of course."

I didn't wait. I walked past him, my shoulder brushing his just enough to feel that cold, otherworldly hum under his skin. Not human. Demon. He'd been with me since the old days. Never named his sins. Never needed to.

I shut the bathroom door behind me. Twisted the faucet. Steam poured over marble like smoke from a dying star. I braced both hands on the sink, staring into the fogging mirror. Red flashed in my eyes, but it was gone in a blink.

I looked... tired. Hollow. I wasn't even pretending anymore.

I dropped the still-lit cigarette in the basin. Stepped under the scalding spray.

And let it burn me clean.

This wasn't temptation. It was sedation. And I was too far gone to care about the difference.

About the Author

Stephanie Pass hails from a tiny Texas town where she lives with her husband, children, and a Boxer dog who talks more than she does. She writes contemporary romance with magical realism and romantasy. Soon, she will dip her toe into some sci-fi romance. She loves books about love, magic, and high fae. She had her own real-life romance story come true when a chance encounter led her to meet her now husband. When she's not writing romance stories, Stephanie is a mom blogger dancing to Taylor Swift at https://thetiptoefairy.com. But you can often find her at the roller skating rink or dancing at the goth nightclubs.

To learn more, join Stephanie's email list :

www.ingramcontent.com/pod-product-compliance
Lightning Source LLC
Chambersburg PA
CBHW071459140726
47997CB00005B/1782